"Do you have a prom... ... ...love?
Raja Prasad ...

I stumble over my sari, but regain my balance before falling on my face. I guess he hasn't heard about my phantom engagement. "I'm uh . . . holding out for my dream man. Or maybe I'll never get married. I don't know. What about you? Are you married?"

"I would not be walking with you here if I were. Although I'm considering prospects."

"You're looking for a wife?"

"She must be an excellent cook, hardworking, willing to care for children and my mother."

I smile while I tuck my heart away for safekeeping. Oh, horror. How could I have thought this man could be perfect?

"My wife must be willing to shoulder many responsibilities with grace."

"What if her shoulders are weak? Maybe she doesn't lift weights."

He chuckles. "Perhaps she also has a sense of humor."

"She'll need one." I clamp a hand over my mouth. Why did I say that?

Imaginary Men

Anjali Banerjee

doWn
tOwn
press

New York London Toronto Sydney

An *Original* Publication of POCKET BOOKS

DOWNTOWN PRESS, published by Pocket Books
1230 Avenue of the Americas
New York, NY 10020

Library of Congress Cataloging-in-Publication Data
Banerjee, Anjali.
    Imaginary men / Anjali Banerjee.—1st Downtown Press
trade pbk. ed.
        p.   cm.
    1. Young women—Fiction. 2. Bengali Americans—Fiction. 3. San Francisco
(Calif.)—Fiction. 4. Conflict of generations—Fiction.
5. Imaginary companions—Fiction. 6. Marriage brokerage—Fiction.
I. Title.
PS3602.A6355I47 2005
813'.6—dc22   2005048441
ISBN-13: 978-1-4165-0943-1
ISBN-10:   1-4165-0943-7

First Downtown Press trade paperback edition October 2005

10 9 8 7 6 5 4 3 2 1

DOWNTOWN PRESS and colophon are
trademarks of Simon & Schuster, Inc.

Manufactured in the United States of America

Designed by Jaime Putorti

For information regarding special discounts for bulk purchases,
please contact Simon & Schuster Special Sales at 1-800-456-6798
or business@simonandschuster.com.

Acknowledgments

I'm grateful to my amazing editor, Maggie Crawford; her assistant, Mara Sorkin; Tara McCarthy; everyone at Pocket Books; and my intrepid agent, Winifred Golden. Thanks also to my astute critiquers: Dotty Sohl, Skip Morris, Jan Symonds, Janine Donoho, Kate Breslin, Lois Dyer, Pj Jough-Haan, Rose Marie Harris, Sandra Hill, Sheila Rabe, Susan Plunkett, Krysteen Seelen, Julie Weston, and Rich Penner.

A heartfelt thank-you to my cousin Kamalini Mukerjee, for describing the Brahmo Samaj wedding ceremony and for reviewing the manuscript. Thanks also to my cousin Sayantoni Palchoudhuri, for information about Bengali wedding rituals. Thanks to Bethel for setting me straight about the Tivoli.

Thank you to Susan Wiggs, for your advice and support, for believing in this book, and for critiquing scenes at the last minute.

ACKNOWLEDGMENTS

Much love and thanks to my parents, Sanjoy Banerjee and Denise Kiser, for their thoughtful input. Thank you to my wonderful husband, Joseph, for your love, your encouragement, and for bringing me meals when I'm working so hard that I forget to eat.

Imagination is the highest kite one can fly.
—Lauren Bacall

Everything you can imagine is real.
—Pablo Picasso

Imaginary Men

One

I'm allergic to India.

I snort and sniff through my sister Durga's wedding, my eyes watering from Kolkata pollution, not because Durga is marrying the Bengali version of Johnny Depp. Not because I'm the eldest sister, twenty-nine and still single.

Sweat seeps through my *choli* shirt, and in this bright turquoise sari, I feel like a giant blueberry. I stand squished among dozens of relatives in an Alipore courtyard at the city's south end. This is Auntie Kiki's home, a two-story mansion in the British colonial style. A hundred guests dressed to the hilt, the women in saris, the men in traditional *dhoti punjabis,* long-sleeved silk shirts with loose trousers. A few bachelors prowl in ill-fitting suits, hair slicked back, cell phones plastered to their ears. I keep my gaze averted. I won't talk to any of these geeks.

Bengali Brahmin weddings often last for days, but Durga's ceremony is Brahmo Samaj, a progressive, secular form of Hinduism that rejects the caste system, child marriages, and the worship of idols. I thank my great-grandparents for embracing the Brahmo Samaj, or I'd be yawning through a thousand rituals.

The scents of coconut oil and sandalwood incense fill the air. Through the crowd, I glimpse my parents sitting near the dais. Onstage, the happy couple exchange garlands as the *acharya,* the priest, chants in Sanskrit. The groom wears a cream-colored punjabi shirt and *dhoti* threaded with gold. Durga is a vision in the red bride's sari, red and white bangles, a heavy gold ring through her nose. Red dye, *alta,* stains her fingers and toes. Black kohl rims her eyes, making her resemble the great Hindu goddess Durga, after whom she was named. She gazes demurely at her feet and pretends to be a shy virgin.

Beside me, Auntie Kiki, all gray hair, uneven yellow teeth, and smiles, lets out a loud sigh and elbows me. "Ah, Lina, you're next, nah? Big Bengali wedding?" She winks, and I wonder, in mild horror, what she has planned.

"I don't know, Auntie. I'm not ready." Men have been nothing but trouble for me, but she won't understand.

"Oh, Vishnu! Nathu dead two years, and still you're not ready?"

"There aren't any good bachelors in California."

She pats my cheek. "You're nearly thirty now. Hadn't you better stop being so picky-choosy?"

"I'm not picky and choosy. I'm discerning."

"*Bhalo.* Good." She nods her head sideways in the Indian style. "We'll find you a husband tonight. I know this."

My insides turn somersaults. What does she mean, *I know this?* What secrets hide in the folds of her sari? Auntie's actually my great-aunt, the eldest of my father's aunts. Her youngest sister, my father's mother, died just before I was born. Because she's the eldest of the female relatives, Auntie Kiki's decisions carry the weight of a queen's formal decree.

"What if I don't want to marry an Indian?" I say.

"What's the matter with Indians? Nathu was Punjabi, nah?"

"Nathu grew up in America. He learned to take out the garbage and make his own bed. He wasn't like traditional Indian men who expect their wives to do everything for them."

"Perhaps it wouldn't hurt you to learn a little tradition." Auntie's lips tighten into a thin line, pulling her cheeks inward.

I'm up to my push-up bra in tradition tonight, I want to say, but I grit my teeth and smile. I know only a few words of

Bengali, and I don't practice Hinduism. What would a true Bengali man think of me? He'd label me damaged goods, spoiled by American decadence.

I glance around the courtyard until I spot my other sister, Kali. I frantically wave at her. *Please, rescue me from Auntie.*

Kali grins and rushes over. "Doesn't Durga look *smashing*?"

"She's beautiful," I say.

"When I find the perfect shagadelic guy, I want a true *desi* wedding, Indian in every way." Loosely translated, *desi* means "of or from my country" in Hindi. Kali's obsessed with the homeland, but she also loves Austin Powers, Man of Mystery. She's young, blooming like a lotus flower. Not that I'm chopped liver, but I don't dress the way she does, all cleavage in a tight-fitting *choli* shirt. She manages to make a sari look like lingerie. I prefer not to draw attention to myself at these shindigs.

I whisper in her ear. "Aren't you seeing a practicing Catholic?"

"I can shop around if I want." She gives me a sly look. "I met someone tonight. His name is Dev. He has mojo. I think I'm in love."

"Kali has no problem meeting bachelors," Auntie says. "It's Lina we must worry about. She's a matchmaker in California and still can't find herself a suitable husband."

"Maybe I'm not looking!"

"We've all been waiting for you to find someone," Kali cuts in. "You're so good at it. You hooked up Durga with her hubby, didn't you?"

"That's different. It's easy to match up other couples." I specialize in hooking up American-born Indian women with their princes. I have an uncanny ability to see connections between potential mates, like silvery threads. But I haven't seen a thread between any man and me since Nathu, and I don't expect to see one tonight.

"Settle down, and you'll not be all the time running around and working," Auntie says. "Why are you so determined to remain unmarried?"

"I'm not determined. I'm *busy*. Besides, I *like* working." I sigh in exasperation. She's talking to Kali about how they have to help poor Lina, the elder sister.

I'm a hopeless case and a disappointment to my family. So what keeps drawing me back to India? Maybe a touch of the exotic, I think as a servant lights flaming torches around the perimeter of the courtyard. Maybe the humid summer climate on the Bay of Bengal. Maybe my Inner Princess expects a mythical prince to gallop through the smog and sweep me off my feet.

Auntie points into the shadows. "There, Lina. Look. Did you meet Nikhil Ghose when you were in Kolkata last?"

"Who?"

One of the suit-clad bachelors appears out of nowhere,

grabs my hand, and squeezes. "Lina Ray? What a complete pleasure to make your acquaintance."

"Likewise, I'm sure." I pull my hand away as politely as possible. I'm staring into the hopeful face of Pee-wee Herman on steroids.

A large woman in a gold sari, stomach folds rippling, barrels toward us. In India, belly rolls are still considered sexy. "Nikhil, son, where are you off to?" she shouts.

Auntie grips my elbow. "This is my accomplished great-niece, Lina. Lina, Nikhil Ghose."

I stiffen, dust stinging my eyes.

"Pleased, pleased," Mrs. Ghose says, nodding sideways.

"Lina plays classical piano and cooks very well," Auntie says. "She's here from America for short time, nah? You must come round for tea."

Dumbfounded, I stare at Auntie. Cooks very well? I can pour milk over Lucky Charms, but Indian food is a mystery. And piano? This is a conspiracy. Auntie must've spoken to Ma, and now they're desperate to arrange my marriage. I'll never agree to a match with Pee-wee. He makes me want to drown myself in the Ganges River.

His mother gives me the once-over, and her lips turn down in a sneer. "She's a bit *thin*, nah? Living in America all this time? Our good girls go thin and wild in America."

"I wasn't raised by wolves," I say.

"She's witty as well," Auntie says.

"I like my women wild." Nikhil gives me a disgusting wink. He even has Pee-wee's voice.

I focus on the ground. He probably thinks I like him and I'm looking down out of shyness.

"Lina's a good girl," Auntie Kiki says. "Fitness craze in America has made her thin. Everyone wants to be slim there. They are doing these exercises, that exercises, all the time jogging, aerobics, spinning, Pirates—"

"Pilates, Auntie," Kali says, smiling. She's going along with this farce.

Nikhil's mother stares hard at me. Gradually, her lips lift at the corners. "Well, we're pleased, of course, that you're *Sahadev* Ray's daughter. *Doctor* Ray's daughter."

"Thank you, Mrs. Ghose." Darn, she traced my lineage. For once, I wish I were a sweeper's child. These things matter in India—whose daughter you are, whose granddaughter you are, who your second cousin twice removed is. Women have goals and dreams, but they often keep them secret, tucked away in their underwear drawers to be worn beneath their clothes, necessary but unseen.

"We shall come for tea, of course. Very pleased." Nikhil's mother is all impressed, my thinness and Americanness forgotten. She turns to Auntie. "The Rays are staying with you? When shall I bring Nikhil?"

He steps closer until I smell his curry breath.

"Tomorrow?" Auntie says.

No, not tomorrow. Not any day. Get me out of here. I'll sit on the curb, contemplate the sewer system, anything but listen to Auntie set me up with Pee-wee. I force a smile and hope the sweat doesn't show through the armpits of my *choli*.

"We'll still be here tomorrow," Kali says. I glare at her.

Nikhil's mother smiles. "Tomorrow shall suit us well. Lina, Nikhil is successful in business, nah? Manufacturing and import-export. He'll give you grand tour of the factories."

"Just the two of us." Nikhil spears me with a lecherous gaze.

My shoulders tense up. "Thanks, but I won't have time. Lots of relatives to visit—"

"Lina!" Auntie shouts. "We'll find the time."

"I really don't think—"

"We'll arrange, nah?" Nikhil's mother resumes reciting his many glowing attributes.

He stands so close, his hot breath sears my cheek. Sweat beads on my brow, and nausea builds in my throat. The *Jaws* theme plays in my mind, and then the answer glows like a rainbow. Of course, of course.

"I have some news," I say.

"News? What is this?" Auntie asks. Her lips tighten.

All goes quiet.

I give a knowing smile. "I was waiting for the right moment, but maybe—" I pause for effect.

Nikhil steps back. His mother blinks.

"What? What's this news?" Auntie's eyes widen. "No, you're not. You're . . . already engaged?"

I nod, although it's a big, fat lie.

"Oh, Vishnu! Why did your Ma not say?" Auntie shouts. "All this time we were arranging your engagement to Nikhil!"

Arranging my engagement? Before I'd even met him? This is worse than I thought.

Tongues cluck and gossip flies. Kali narrows her gaze. Perhaps she sees through my deception. "Is this true?"

"Yes, it's true. My fiancé is quite high up." I gaze into the dusty, darkening sky. "Accomplished. Rich. Very handsome. Gentlemanly and a bit dangerous." I'm already beginning to picture him in my mind. He looks a lot like Nathu.

Oohs and aahs.

"Is he Indian?" Kali asks a question the others wouldn't bother to pose. They just assume.

"In a manner of speaking," I say. "He's the perfect man."

"What does he look like?"

"Tall. Dark, wavy hair. The most beautiful eyes—he's a dream."

"Sounds a little too perfect," Kali says.

"Why is this man not with you?" Nikhil snaps.

"He travels all the time. Here and there. Riding elephants into the jungle, touring his palaces, several properties—"

"How can you stand being away from him?" Kali asks. "Don't you miss him terribly?"

"Like the devil." I sigh. "But he sends postcards."

"E-mails? Love letters?"

I nod. "He embeds photos and poems in the messages—"

"All this was happening, and you didn't tell?"

I smile. "Isn't the Internet amazing?"

Mrs. Ghose huffs. "Come, Nikhil." She grabs his arm and yanks him away in search of another victim. My shoulders relax.

Auntie nearly swoons. "Congratulations are in order. We must summon your parents—"

"They don't know yet," I say quickly. "It's a love match, not arranged."

"They don't know?" Auntie's eyebrows rise, and her cheeks puff outward.

"Things are different in America. Parents don't chaperone their daughters on dates."

"Ah, yes, this can't be helped. All the same, this is good news. Marriage is marriage. Is it an auspicious match?"

"I believe the stars are aligned just right."

"Who is he? What's his name?" Kali asks.

"It's a surprise. He'll be traveling for . . . a few more weeks." With every lie, I dig a deeper hole. I might as well climb in and let the dirt fall on top of me.

Auntie clasps and unclasps her hands. She's in planning mode. "I must meet this man and make sure he is more suitable than Nikhil."

"More suitable? I already know he is—"

"*I* must know!"

"Of course, Auntie. Your approval will honor me."

She smoothes her ruffled sari. "*Bhalo.* You'll bring him to India?"

Bring him? "He has business in San Francisco."

How will I maintain this charade? Soon I'll have to say Mr. Perfect and I have split up. He found a girlfriend in Germany or Italy, on his travels. He'll go when I want him to go. But I can't marry Pee-wee. What to do?

"You'll bring him to India for a Bengali wedding, of course," Auntie says.

"When the time comes." No matter how long we've lived in America, we must return to India for this rite of passage.

I slip into the house to the bathroom. I lean my elbows on the sink and focus on breathing. In through the nose, out through the mouth. I can't afford to have a panic attack here, in a Kolkata bathroom with a concrete floor and old-fashioned toilet with a chain hanging down.

I gaze into the mirror, at the black kohl smudged beneath my eyes. My hair, cut to my shoulders, is frizzy in the humidity.

"Lina, Lina, on the wall," I say to my reflection, then let out a crazy giggle. "Who's the biggest liar of them all?"

Two

I pull myself together and return to the courtyard in time to witness the *sindoor daan*. Durga's handsome groom applies the symbol of marriage to her hair part: a red stain of henna called the *sindoor*. If she's a good Hindu woman, she'll wear this symbol until her death.

Durga has a *sindoor* now. Ah well, who wants to wear henna on her scalp all the time and endure Americans asking, Why do you have blood in your hair? Did you cut your head?

I'm happy for her. May she and her groom, Amit, live a long and blissful life, have many tall, fair-skinned children—

all of whom will be married off before the age of twenty—
and live happily ever after.

The bride and groom rise to take the traditional seven
steps together.

Auntie returns to my side. "Ah, the *saptapadi*!" she whispers in my ear. Her breath emits the odor of garlic. "Step one
pays homage to the Almighty, the next is a promise of coop-
eration, the third a promise of discipline. The fourth is a
promise to discover joy, the fifth is for the sake of children,
the sixth is for family prosperity, and the seventh is for the
blessing of mutual company."

"Why don't they just dance as they do in Hindi movies?" I
say. I like the promise to discover joy, but I'd gladly discard
the other six steps. The wedding ceremony ends, and the
bride and groom kneel to touch the feet of their elders.

There's a rush as relatives and friends gather to bestow
their blessings. I weave through the crowd and hug Durga,
who exudes the scents of sweat and jasmine perfume.

"Congratulations, sweetie. Long life together and much
happiness." I hold her warm hands in mine.

Tears brighten her eyes. "Thank you, Didi, and now
you're the one who should be congratulated. Finally engaged.
I thought you were too scared!" She kisses my cheeks. She has
always called me Didi, "elder sister."

I'm in such trouble now. "I'm not marrying Pee-wee—I
mean, Nikhil Ghose. Just so we have that straight, right?"

"Of course you're not. But he must be devastated, nah? You have a mystery man!"

"News travels fast in India." I was in the bathroom for all of five minutes.

"Everyone knows. Congratulations." Amit shakes my hand with his large one. Close up, he looks even more like Johnny Depp with a permanent tan.

"Thanks, I think."

"You and your fiancé must visit us in our new house!" Durga says.

"When I'm ready for the boondocks."

She and Amit live in a protected suburb of Los Angeles, where lawns unfold like perfect green napkins. "Why don't you move to San Francisco, near me?"

"Is the city any place to raise children, Lina? What with gangs and burglaries—"

"I've never had a problem. I have a view of Coit Tower and the city lights. I can even go out on the roof." I don't go on the roof too often these days. Roofs are romantic places made for two.

"When you marry, you may have to move," Durga says. "Children need playgrounds, not views. You can't have them falling off the roof."

"I haven't thought that far ahead." My skin prickles with irritation. I don't have a real man, and already she's talking about children.

"The time is coming sooner than you think, nah?" Amit winks as we're carried along on a current of guests heading inside for the reception.

In the dining room on the first floor, Auntie has spread a feast on long tables—rice and *dahl,* curry and potatoes, and sweet *roshogollas* for dessert. I hide in the crowd, but Ma finds me in a heartbeat. She's slim, with a moon-shaped face and frizzy hair like mine. She looks truly Indian in her traditional green sari, the *bindi* on her forehead; you'd never know she wears jeans to the university in Santa Barbara, where she teaches mechanical engineering.

"My little girl is leaving. The full impact is just now hitting, nah?" She presses a hand to her chest as if damming a torrent of tears.

"You can visit them in boondockville."

Ma shakes her head. "What's your mother supposed to feel when her daughter is married? Is she not supposed to shed tears of joy and grief?"

"I'm sorry. It's been a trying day. All the festivities. I hope this goes off well, or people will accuse me of setting up a bad match."

"Finally, you've found a good match for yourself too." Ma touches my cheek. "Ah, Lina. After Nathu, I never thought—"

"Ma—" I take her hand from my cheek and hold her cool fingers in mine. I want to tell her I lied. I want to explain, but the words won't come.

"How could you keep this from your mother? Auntie Kiki and Uncle Gula came and gave congratulations, and I was pretending to know all about your fiancé. Lucky I'm a good actress."

A skill I inherited. "I was planning to tell you, Ma." I step away and grab a *roshogolla* from the table.

"Baba's indigestion has returned, you know. Ulcer last winter, and he never fully recovered. This news will make him well."

"I'm glad." I nod and smile as relatives go by, but my stomach turns upside down. Baba's health problems worry me.

"We're so happy for you." Ma's eyes shine with concentrated joy, and I don't have the heart to undo my lie. "What's his name?"

"It's a secret for the moment."

"A secret? Why? What does his father do? Does he come from a good family? Does he make enough money to support you?"

"He makes loads of money—"

"Good. You'll tell all."

"Not now, Ma. Later. We must entertain the guests."

"Then soon, nah?" She leaves me with fake answers on my tongue and flits off to join my father, a half-balding man talking to the groom's father.

I can handle Baba from a distance. He resembles any other Indian father-of-the-bride, puffing with pride. And I can handle him at his office, where he wears a white coat and stethoscope, jots prescriptions, and orders the nurses around. When he tries to order me around, my fingers curl into fists and my jaw clenches. His bushy brows gather like a storm, the tightness in his lips saying I've failed him.

I wonder what he thinks of me now. What would he do if he knew the truth? He would disown me; tell everyone he never had a daughter named Lina.

I turn away and find myself trapped among a group of aunts peppering me with questions. I deflect the nosiness with my best vague lies. My stomach churns. I escape to the room where the younger set congregates. Someone cranks up a Bollywood pop song, a high-pitched Hindi soprano over a repetitive synthetic backbeat. Women slip off their sandals and drag their husbands onto the dance floor. Kali dances with a handsome man with long hair tied back in a ponytail. I wonder if this is her Dev. Bellies gyrate, and Pee-wee cuts through the crowd toward me, a piece of mint leaf wedged between his two front teeth.

Didn't he get the message? I'm off-limits, taken, spoken for, practically hitched.

"One dance?" he asks in his nasal voice. "You'll not have another chance to be a swinger."

"I'm . . . feeling too sick to swing." I try not to stare at the green leaf in his teeth.

"Come, come. You'll change your mind about your fiancé

ANJALI BANERJEE

when you dance with me." He grabs my hands, but I yank
them away and rush outside into the courtyard.

I should dance with Pee-wee, try to make the best of the
festivities, for Durga's sake. I should celebrate my sister's marriage, only I don't belong. Why? Because my own fiancé died
two years ago, left me with unfinished dreams and half-
formed wishes? Anger wells in my throat. I stride away from
the house, away from the laughter.

Only the servants are here, clearing cups and crumbs from
the ground. Flaming torches flicker around the courtyard,
sending fingers of shadow across the grass.

I cross my arms over my chest, hunch against the damp-
ness, and hurry out to the lane. My lies pursue me like chattering ghosts. I'll lose myself along the street between houses.
I need time to think.

Threads of distant music drift out into the night. I'm
light-years from my family. I glance back at Auntie's mansion,
its window-eyes gazing out with indifference.

Then I turn and leave it all behind. The farther I go, the
quieter the night becomes. The occasional bird rustles and twit-
ters in the shrubbery. Pollution bathes the sky in surreal orange.
Hard to believe that a city with over a hundred thousand people per square mile can snap into silence at nightfall. Anything
could wait around the bend—a monkey, a cobra, a python.

Or a man.

I bump into him as he strides around the corner.

Three

"Excuse me," I say.

He's tall, maybe one of the wedding guests. He wears a *dhoti punjabi* and holds a scruffy gray kitten in the crook of his elbow. I tilt my head back to look up into his face, and I gape like an idiot.

His shoulders are broad, his lips full, his eyelashes long. The hint of a beard shadows his jaw. His eyes glint, almost menacing. Omigod, I've been flipping through too many romance novels.

He resembles the Hindu god Krishna, trickster and renowned lover. A thin scar forms an upside-down half-moon on his left cheek. A battle scar. I imagine him mounting a black stallion, drawing his sword, racing off to combat. What am I thinking? Nobody fights with swords these days. We're not in Middle Earth. He probably nicked himself shaving. Okay, instead, he throws me over his shoulder and carries me off to his lair, only we're ten thousand years past all that, too.

His gaze sweeps over me. I'm an escaped prisoner in the spotlight. "Are you lost, ma'am? What are you doing wandering from the party by yourself?" His voice is deep, with a cultured accent.

"You were at the wedding too? At Kiki's?"

He nods, skewering me with his gaze. "I'm a friend of a friend of the groom. Six degrees of separation."

"I see. I came out to see the stars at twilight, but I can't see anything through the smog." I smooth down my hair.

"This is not the best viewing time. Wait until after astronomical twilight."

"You're an astronomer?" He's not carrying binoculars or a telescope. Only a kitten.

"My family sells granite overseas. India is the number-one stone exporter in the world."

"I didn't know—"

"But I have a special interest in the stars. Did you know there are three different moments of twilight? Civil twilight, nautical twilight, and astronomical twilight."

And I've spent my life thinking the sun rose and set in its predictable, cyclical way. "Which one is happening now?"

"The beginning of nautical twilight. General outlines are still visible, but the horizon is indistinct."

"Fascinating!" I bite my lip. I might've drawn blood. "Is that your kitten?"

"I found her in a tree. I'll take her home and give her some food. Shall we walk?" He offers his free arm. "I'm Raja Prasad, and you are—"

"Lina Ray. The bride is my sister." The name *Raja* means "king" in Sanskrit. He acts more like the formal Mr. Darcy in *Pride and Prejudice*.

I'm Elizabeth Bennet taking his arm, although I look nothing like her. I'm a sun-browned version in a billowing sari.

I catch a whiff of exotic aftershave, wildness hidden beneath Raja's civilized exterior. I walk fast to keep up with his long, easy strides.

"Ah, you're Durga's sister. You live in the States, then?"

"We traveled a lot for my mother's job. She's a professor. We all live in different parts of California now."

"I've been to San Francisco, Seattle, New York, Los Angeles. Beautiful country. My younger brother will finish his MBA at Berkeley this year."

"My alma mater. I live in San Francisco."

"Then he must look you up." Raja raises an eyebrow.

ANJALI BANERJEE

I feel his gaze on my profile. I hope there's no snot hanging from my nose, but I'm afraid to wipe. I don't have a tissue, and my eyes still water from the dust and smog. I'm casual, cool. I won't trip over my sari. "Yes, of course. I'll give you my number. I mean, I'll have my father give the number to your brother. You know."

"Of course. You live alone in the city?"

"For now, yes. I have a good job there."

"What type of business?"

"I work for Lakshmi Matchmakers."

"Lakshmi, the goddess of love?" His eyebrows rise. "You're a matchmaker? You don't strike me as the type."

"What do you mean, 'the type'?"

"Matchmakers socialize. But you're out here walking alone—"

"Matchmaking is different in America. More . . . anonymous. Much can be done over the Internet."

"How did you choose such a profession?"

"I fell into it. In university, I learned about measurement and personality profiles, and then I realized I was able to predict who would end up together in my dormitory."

"Remarkable. The parents trust you?"

"Why wouldn't they? I'm usually right. I measure body language; the way couples talk to each other. I have a sharp eye for detail. Quite mathematical, really."

"Ah, so you're a scientist."

"You could say that. I'm not your typical matchmaker."

"How do you know when the match is right?"

"I find two people who fit each other's requirements. Age, interests, family background. If they're Indian. Not all my clients are. Then I get a sense of whether the couple has a rapport. They should laugh together. Laughter's important."

"That doesn't sound mathematical."

"I start with the math, then I resort to intuition." I want to tell him about the silvery threads, but this would sound silly even to me. *You see, a shimmering filament sprouts from a man's chest and reaches out to latch on to the woman. Then I know the two are meant for each other.*

"So you agree that in the end, love cannot be quantified?"

The kitten has fallen asleep in Raja Prasad's arms, one paw extended. "No, I suppose not, but . . . Sometimes it's love at first sight. Sometimes there's just the promise of love."

He studies me with intensity, as if he's holding a magnifying glass between us. "What about you? Do you have a promise of love?"

I stumble over my sari, but regain my balance before falling on my face. I guess he hasn't heard about my phantom engagement. "I'm, uh . . . holding out for my dream man. Or maybe I'll never get married. I don't know. What about you? Are you married?"

"I would not be walking with you here if I were. Although I'm considering prospects."

"You're looking for a wife?"

"She must be an excellent cook, hardworking, willing to care for children and my mother."

Children? His mother? Next, he'll want a slave to serve his entire extended family. I imagine I'm Cinderella scrubbing the floor while his evil mother yells at me. She's the size of a Sherman tank, with twenty rolls of fat on her belly. How would I care for her? I can barely care for myself. On busy days, I forget to eat breakfast.

I smile while I tuck my heart away for safekeeping. Oh, horror. How could I have thought this man could be perfect?

"What about your father?" I ask. "Doesn't he take care of the family?"

"He died some years back."

"Oh, I'm sorry." I look at the ground. Why am I tongue-tied?

"Thank you. So, you see, my wife must be willing to shoulder many responsibilities with grace."

"What if her shoulders are weak? Maybe she doesn't lift weights."

He chuckles. "Perhaps she also has a sense of humor."

"She'll need one." Raja might be dashing on the outside, but on the inside, he's sexist.

I hold fast to the image of my ideal fiancé. He'll rub my shoulders after my long day at work. He'll make dinner. He knows my cooking skill extends to heating up organic cheese enchiladas in the microwave. He loves me all the same, nurtures me, nourishes me, but this Raja Prasad—

"But you know," he says, "perhaps the only thing I really want is a best friend, a lover, someone with whom to share my life."

"No, what you want is a Stepford Wife." I clamp a hand over my mouth. Why did I say that?

"Perhaps. We'll see."

"I'm sure you'll have no trouble finding the perfect woman."

Kali's melodic voice breaks through the night. She's calling me from the house.

I disengage my hand from Raja's elbow. "I should be getting back."

"Wait. I have something for you." He digs into his pocket and produces a black stone the size of a robin's egg. "This type of granite is called Star Galaxy."

"You needn't—"

"Consider it a reminder of India." He gazes into my eyes as if to say, Consider it a reminder of me.

"That's very kind, but I have nothing to give you." I take the stone, flecked with white spots. It feels warm and smooth in the palm of my hand. I catch another whiff of his cologne, and a flicker of awareness passes through me.

"You've already given me your friendship," he says. "And your candor. Honesty is of great value to me."

"Thank you." Ha! Me, honest? If only he knew.

"If you decide to return to India, bring the stone back to its home by the sea. Now I must take the cat to the car. Good evening."

"Good evening." I give the cat's head a quick pet, then turn and run back to the house in the rising wind. Good evening? Nobody says "Good evening" any more. They say it only in old movies like *Casablanca*.

"Lina, where have you been?" Kali rushes onto the veranda. "We've been looking for you."

"I met a man. He's a chauvinist. Good thing I'm already engaged." I don't mention Star Galaxy.

"Where'd he go?" She squints into the darkness.

"Into oblivion, I hope."

Inside, the atmosphere is subdued as the bride and groom prepare to leave with the groom's family. I go to the drawing room and drop the stone in my handbag. There's no sign of Raja Prasad as we all file back outside and bid the happy couple teary good-byes. After the honeymoon in Goa, on the west coast of India, they'll return to their software jobs in California.

"Don't do anything I wouldn't do." Kali throws her arms around Durga's neck. They both burst into tears.

"I'll be back, don't go saying this is forever." Although the youngest, Durga is the tallest of the three of us, muscular and big-boned like our father. She holds herself with a sporty air, bouncing with every step.

Kali is voluptuous, creamy-skinned, a wannabe Bolly-wood actress with the quick temper of the formidable goddess Kali, killer of demons. I got Ma's slim limbs, dark complexion, and passion for reading.

I hug Durga and then the groom. "Be good to my sister. She takes lots of milk in her tea, and three cubes of sugar. And she snores and sometimes falls off the bed—"

"I know. Not to worry." Amit wraps his arms around Durga. "Now we must plan *your* wedding."

I wave him away, but a lump rises in my throat as I watch the groom's wedding party fold into hulking Ambassador cars. Durga will cook breakfast tomorrow for Amit's family, to stake her place in the household. But times have changed. She won't live with his family in Kolkata. If she did, she would fall under the iron hand of his mother.

Kali grabs my arm. "I'm going to miss her, Didi. I hope this is right."

"They can always get a divorce." But I know Durga is the most traditional sister of the three of us. She will hang on to this marriage until her fingers bleed, no matter how bad things get.

"When I marry, it'll be for keeps," Kali says. "Maybe it'll be the cool cat I met tonight."

"The long-haired guy?"

"Don't tell, nah? He says he'll call me."

"Long distance? So I guess the Catholic guy is out of the picture."

She nods, and I roll my eyes. Kali prefers impossible long-distance relationships.

The other guests trickle away, congratulating my father and patting him on the back. Could it be this easy, letting go of my youngest sister? Durga will return to America, but she'll be different. She'll be a married woman with obligations. A husband, children, a house, henna in her hair part.

I've lost her.

Ma wipes tears from her eyes, and Baba goes back into the house with Auntie's husband. Auntie smiles. "I did a fine job of planning this wedding, nah?"

Ma pats her arm. "You're always in fine form."

Auntie grips my elbow with talonlike fingers. "Remember, once I've approved the match, we'll plan your wedding."

"We were hoping for a more private ceremony," I start to say, but my throat dries up.

There's a silence, then she says, "Only thirty, forty people then. Maybe fifty. Very private wedding. And tomorrow I will take you to see Pandit Parsai."

"Auntie. I don't need to see an astrologer! We don't believe in such things—"

"Nah, nah, we must. He's been advising me for years. When you were just a baby, I had him write up your natal horoscope."

No, please! I read the horoscope in the newspaper every morning, but I don't take it seriously. Now Auntie wants me to consult her Pandit about a fiancé who doesn't exist. "Auntie, remember what you said? Pandit predicted I'd search across the world for love. Look at me. I stayed in San Francisco."

"Do not speak ill of Pandit Parsai!" Auntie shouts. "He predicts everything with great accuracy—illness, good fortune, and marriage. I'll give him a ring tonight, and we'll see him first thing tomorrow."

Four

You're rarely alone in India.

I run upstairs to the bedroom I share with Kali. There's no door, only a silk curtain hanging in an archway, but the illusion of privacy slows my heartbeat. I peel off my clothes and change into Victoria's Secret flannel pajamas. Relief. Any moment, a relative will stride in unannounced, but for now, I can breathe. How I miss solid doors with brass knobs and deadbolts.

I've been here only three days. Jetlag turns my insides upside down. My digital clock reads 10:00 P.M., yet my stomach growls for breakfast. My hosts would be insulted if I asked for cereal right after the wedding feast, and now that I've lied, I couldn't even choke down my beloved Lucky Charms. My stomach has no room for anything but shame, and a dull headache squeezes my temples.

Besides, nobody eats cereal in India. We'll have *parathas* and *dahl* in the morning, with mango slices. India is the land of mushy food—rice, *dahl*, curry. Everything is soft and yellow.

A horn beeps, and a man shouts in Hindi. Heavy air rife with pollution and smoke curls up beneath the high ceiling. I untuck the mosquito net from the mattress and flop on the bed, a four-poster as old as the Taj Mahal. The mosquito net's white gauze lends a surreal fuzziness to the walls painted in jungle green, stained with watermarks from the humidity. A grayish house gecko, a lizard the size of a large mouse, clings to the windowsill. Vertical pupils widen ominously.

Geckos are harmless, I tell myself in a mantra. They won't slither under the sheets. They won't crawl over my face and bite my nose. They've shared Indian homes for centuries. They've watched mothers give birth, elders die. They've flicked their tongues at foreigners like me, stumbling witless through an alien country.

I was born here, but who remembers infancy? My parents whisked me to America before I could say "Ma." Yet my soul connects to this strange, colorful, hot, smelly, magical country, even though I don't remember it. Do all Indians share a collective memory? Culture imprinted in our DNA? Is that why I lied, because in a tiny corner of my heart, I belong here?

What a terrifying thought. Me, Lina Ray, poster child for independence, settling in India with a husband, a family? Impossible.

Auntie's daughters left home to reside with their husbands' families. Her son, his wife, and their baby boy live here, on the first floor. Before the wedding, they escaped to their Darjeeling tea gardens. I wish I could follow, hop the train to the Himalayas along cliff edges and switchbacks, away from family expectations. Away from the chaos of Kolkata, the hum of gossip drifting in from the living room. Away from my lies. I could reveal the truth, but Ma's excitement permeates the house. I've never seen her so happy, not even when Durga announced her engagement. I've finally made my mother proud. Now what am I going to do?

Kali bursts in and plunks down on the bed. She leans in toward me, gives off pungent aromas of sandalwood and sweat. "So tell me now. Have you slept with him?"

"Slept with whom—Oh, him! What do *you* think? I'm not saving myself for marriage, Kali."

Her eyelashes flutter as she lets out a low whistle. "Is he good in bed? Better than Nathu?"

"Kali, please, not here—"

"I can't wait to meet him! You're flushed. Shiny eyes, the works. Now I know why. You've been getting some."

I'm developing a fever. Maybe I've caught a bug. I accidentally drank ice water tonight, another mistake. Although Auntie purifies her drinking water, the ice might come from unboiled tap water.

Kali glances toward the doorway. "Brace yourself for the elders."

I sit up straight. "What, now? But—"

"You're engaged. Shagadelic! You get the gold. I am *so* jealous."

Newly engaged women receive gifts of gold from their elders. I get the gold, and I haven't even trained for the Olympics. I deserve to be disqualified. Why didn't I consider this when I created my imaginary man?

Auntie and Ma march in, saris swishing. They're holding black Kashmiri boxes painted in intricate paisley patterns. The bed will collapse beneath the weight of all four of us.

In the living room, the men drown their boredom in laughter and whisky. There's nowhere to hide, unless I jump out the window, and then hundreds of concerned passersby will converge on my bloodied corpse. My ghost will find no peace in the crowds.

"My dearest Pupu," Ma says, patting my cheek.

I wince at the sound of my childhood pet name. In our family, everyone has a pet name and a given name. Lucky for me, my pet name fell out of favor as I grew older. Until now.

Ma's eyes glisten with tears. "You've made me happier than words can say. You've finally found the life I dreamed for you. Where will you live when you're married? You'll come to Santa Barbara?"

Yikes. Now what? "We'll cross that bridge when we come to it," I say.

Auntie rests a pudgy hand on my knee. Her nails are long and painted red. Heavy gold rings squeeze her fingers. She must've slipped on the rings years ago, when she was slim, and then never took them off. "It's never too soon to plan," she says. "We must make a list of wedding guests. If we forget anyone, God forbid, we shall never hear the end of it."

Kali nods in solemn collusion. "It's so important to get this right. We don't want to shame the family, especially given the status of your beloved. You know how people gossip. The Gangulis invited us to their son's wedding. You have to invite them. And Mira Das. Remember her?"

"I met her once, in San Francisco."

"She invited us to her wedding, and you must invite her to yours."

"I didn't go. I can't fly to India ten times a year, at the drop of a hat, for all the weddings!"

"Lina, really!" Ma says.

Auntie clears her throat. Her thick, busy fingers pull at the end of her sari.

"Oh, Kali, I'm sorry," I say. "I didn't mean to snap. I'm just tired."

She pats my knee. "Must be overwhelming, to be engaged. We'll make the guest list later."

I can't keep track of the family's vast net of acquaintances. They'll all come to the wedding between me and a phantom, a gold-embroidered *dhoti punjabi* with no man inside. I turn to Auntie. "Look, no need to do all that work."

"Let me give you some advice," Auntie says. "We plan. We're women. It's what we do. Better to have a plan, even if things change down the road. What will be, will be, nah? Your beloved will understand. Once you're married, let him believe he's making all the decisions. Usually, he won't know what he's talking about."

I play with my earring, twisting and twisting, a habit when I'm nervous.

The gecko climbs over the windowsill into the room and crawls along the wall.

"Lina knows how to take care of things," Ma says. "She always did. Even as a child, she smoothed over Kali's naughtiness. If Kali broke a glass, Lina cleaned up the mess. You didn't think I knew, but I knew. My Lina, such a ray of sunshine. She never lets us down."

Kali squeezes my arm. "You were the smart one, always helping me with homework, reading to me."

The gecko creeps across the wall toward us. Nobody seems to notice.

Auntie claps. "*Acha*, it's true. I came to stay. Do you remember, Lina? You were about seven."

35

"How could I forget?" I picture Auntie standing at the stove, cooking basmati rice, her hair twisted into a braid down her back. She must've stayed for months while Ma disappeared to university for her doctorate. The scent of Auntie's curry sank into the upholstery, the linoleum floors. She created a tiny shrine to the elephant god, Ganesh, in the guest room, although in Brahmo Samaj tradition, she's not supposed to worship idols.

"You introduced me to your imaginary friends," Auntie says. "Little animals with whom you had tea parties."

Heat creeps up my neck. "I read *Alice in Wonderland*."

"You got along better with your made-up friends than you did with your real ones," Ma says. "You often played by yourself with your stuffed animals. Kali, however, brought her friends over for fashion shows. They tried on all my lipsticks and high-heeled shoes. She wanted to be a fashion model from babyhood. She would've worn designer diapers."

We burst into laughter.

"Durga was the athlete," Ma goes on. "Always on the track team and playing this sport and that sport. Ah, Durga . . ." Her eyes glaze, and I know she's thinking of her youngest daughter, asleep beneath a mosquito net in a strange house on the other side of the city. Well, maybe not asleep, if she and Amit steal any privacy.

"Lucky Durga found a husband who doesn't mind her

build," Auntie says. "Too much muscle, and she'll look like a man."

Kali and I trade knowing glances. No use trying to set Auntie straight. She's old world.

"Durga's beautiful," I say. "She was lovely at the wedding, and Amit's a good man."

"*Acha*. Now *you* will have a good man, nah?" Auntie opens her Kashmiri box. Inside, a golden bangle lies on a bed of red satin. Each end of the bangle forms a curved serpent head, with tiny eyes of inlaid ruby.

Kali gasps, a sharp pinprick of sound.

My throat tightens.

"My grandmother gave this to my mother," Auntie says, "who gave it to me. Now it's yours." Her voice grows husky.

Ma wipes a tear from her cheek. Her lips tremble.

"No, you mustn't. Auntie—" Silly me. I'm choked with emotion. "You should give this to Durga. She's already married."

"*Acha*, I've already given. This bangle is reserved for the *eldest* daughter." She removes the bracelet from its satin bed and slips it onto my wrist. The cold metal sends a shiver up my arm. The gecko crawls closer until I can see the tiny bumps on its scaly skin.

"Ah, lovely," Ma says. "Gold suits you."

"Fits," says Kali. "You have a narrow wrist. Mine's too thick."

"Beautiful, Auntie," I say, "I don't deserve it. Please, keep the bangle for Kali."

"I have other gifts for Kali," Auntie says. "I insist you keep this. Family heirloom passed through the generations. It can only belong to you upon your engagement. As it belonged to me upon mine."

"Thank you, Auntie. I'll cherish it forever."

"*Acha*—our Lina, all grown up." Auntie does the sideways head nod, and her face goes slack. She looks vulnerable, like a little girl. I picture her in a dress, running in the courtyard, pigtails flying out behind her. She was young and slim and carefree once.

Ma's fingers tremble as she opens her box. Inside, a gold brooch shines in the shape of a lotus leaf. "My mother gave this to me. So now you have one gift from your great-aunt on your Baba's side, one from me."

Tears well up in my throat. "Ma, I can't take it. You've had that brooch for years. You wore it to the wedding!"

"Don't argue." She pins the brooch to my shirt, nearly impaling my breast. "Only for you when you're engaged."

"Ma, how can I thank you?" I envelop her in a tight hug. Her shoulders feel bony. How could my mother have become so small? So fragile? I let go of her and sit back against the headboard. How can I go on lying to her?

The gecko grips the bedpost now. Black eyes regard me with a fathomless gaze. The lizard knows the truth. It's just waiting for me to speak.

"I'm not really getting married," I say.

"*Acha*, it must seem unreal," Auntie says. "After all this time, to have actually found—"

"You don't understand. I'm not—really—getting married."

Ma blows her nose into a Kleenex tissue. "Don't change your mind now. No getting cold feet. Not after we've told everyone."

"You've told everyone, already? But there's no fiancé. I made him up. I can't take your jewelry."

Ma pats my cheek. "Engagement can be overwhelming, but you'll adjust, nah? Take one step at a time."

The golden brooch reflects the light, throwing an elongated triangle of white across the wall. The gecko is gone.

Kali drapes her arm around my shoulders. "You've always denied yourself true happiness, Lina. You were always taking care of your two younger sisters. Now I'm telling you, don't turn your back on bliss. You deserve it."

Ma, Auntie, and Kali bathe me in their joy and tears, and I'm happy and miserable at the same time. They think all is right with the world. I'm a charlatan, the Great Pretender.

The ruby serpent eyes glitter on my wrist. I half expect the creature to come to life and flick out its tongue. The gecko has disappeared, and the snake has taken its place, as vivid as the lie I told.

Five

$\mathcal{I}$ wake up sweating. My nightshirt is soaked. The mosquito net undulates around me. Merchants shout in the street outside, and the smoky odor of cow dung drifts into my nose. I lie still, taking in the peculiar angle of morning light, the curved, high ceiling, and Auntie's echoing voice as she talks to Ma and Kali in the dining room. After three trips back to India, I'm still a stranger here. Then my heart sinks as I remember—I'm going to see Pandit Parsai today.

I sit up and rub sleep from my eyes. My limbs and eyelids are heavy. My tongue swells with thirst. I miss my apartment, the windows with screens, the newspaper outside my door every morning. San Francisco is an ache in my chest, a memory of fresh ocean air, clean streets, privacy, no mosquito nets, no dust.

I have the chills. I'm getting sick. Parasites worm their way into my stomach and remind me I don't belong here. My body has gone soft from the easy life in America. I could never survive here, with malaria and dysentery roaming the streets like criminals waiting for the next foreign victim.

I untuck the mosquito net and step down onto the cold concrete floor, unknown territory. The gecko could be hiding under the bed. I scuttle to the bathroom, then gasp when I catch a reflection in the mirror. Someone else slipped in here with me, a dark-skinned, bright-eyed woman with tangled hair. Omigod, that's me.

The astrologer will think Auntie plucked a wild ape from the jungle, draped clothes on her, and brought her home to the family. A new pet.

At least the bathroom has a door, although there's no lock. I'm nearly out of toilet paper. There's no paper dispenser by the toilet, only a water tap, which I'll never learn to use. People here master the art of self-washing from day one. I vaguely remember my two-year-old niece screaming as her Ma tried to teach her to wash. By the time she turned four, the practice had become second nature for her.

My relatives probably think American customs are filthy. Wiping with toilet paper? No washing? Here, the paper rolls are thin and expensive—maybe a few American dollars per roll—and the tissue as rough as sandpaper. Each roll is encased in a secret unmarked wrap, like contraband. Or an artifact. I imagine toilet paper under glass at the local museum, labeled as a perverse American curiosity.

I use the last few squares. Maybe I'll find some crumpled Kleenex tissue in my luggage. I hope.

Then I get in the shower, the lukewarm water trickling from the showerhead in an annoying thin stream. Cold water pools on the floor, and the threadbare white towel isn't thick enough to wipe it up. It takes me twenty minutes to get my body marginally clean, and I'm even more convinced that I'll never belong in this country. I'm a slave to creature comforts.

After breakfast, Auntie and I squeeze into the Ambassador bound for Pandit Parsai's flat near New Market, in the city center. We wind along narrow, bumpy roads choked with Ambassador taxis, buses, tongas, bullock carts, and jaywalkers. I hold my nose against the reek of burning cow dung and exhaust. Grime settles in every pore of my skin. Our driver, a fearless, brown-skinned Evel Knievel, hurtles through traffic, jolting to a stop, yelling at crowds congregating in the streets. A cacophony of car horns blares against the onslaught of pedestrians, mangy white dogs, and the occasional bony cow.

My heart flits like a hummingbird. The damp air plasters

my shirt to my back. Just riding through the city is an exercise in fortitude. I'd rather visit the elegant Victoria Memorial—built to honor Queen Victoria—the botanical gardens, or the Birla planetarium. I'd rather do anything but see Pandit Parsai.

Kali escaped to Chowringhee Bazaar to buy saris. She knew if she came with me, the pandit would predict her future, too. Ma and Baba went to visit a second cousin named Sugar or Sweetie or Sweet'n Low—I can't keep track of my relatives' nicknames. My parents don't consult astrologers, but they've left me at Auntie's mercy.

She's adorned in a woven golden silk sari. She washed her hair with the Head and Shoulders shampoo I brought from San Francisco. The clean scent mixes with Armani perfume, which I grabbed at a duty-free shop in Heathrow Airport.

Auntie tugs the collar of my blouse. "Why are you wearing these Western clothes, Lina? Pants and top? Why no *salwar*?"

I rarely wear a *salwar kameez,* the long, fashionable top over billowing pants, which makes me resemble a shapeless amoeba.

I was careful to wear the golden bracelet she gave me last night, and I pinned Ma's golden brooch to my shirt. "Pandit should see me in my regular Western clothes."

"This way of dressing is normal in the States, I suppose. No jewelry?"

"I don't want to wear a neon sari and a hundred bangles."
Women here could direct traffic with their brightly colored
clothes. "Oh, I'm sorry, Auntie. I'm just nervous."

"Nothing to be nervous about." She pats my knee. "Last
night, I gave Pandit all of your beloved's information, except
his name, of course. We must have his name."

"It's a secret, until he returns from his travels. All I gave
you was his birth date!" I made up a date that includes threes,
after the three forms of twilight.

"And much more, nah? Profession, hobbies. Have you got
a snap of him?"

"All my photos are at home." A calf ambles across the
road, followed by a few squawking chickens. The driver hits
the horn several times in staccato succession.

"Does your beloved have a natal chart?" Auntie asks.

"He comes from a family of astronomers. They're interested in science, not astrology. Black holes and galaxies and
forms of twilight."

Auntie frowns. "Vedic astrology *is* a science, Lina. He had
no horoscope reading? He must've received one at birth. No
diagrams of the Rasi Chakra, the Shodasavarga charts, the
planetary periods—"

"Nothing like that. I doubt his parents even have an astrologer."

"Such a shame. Well, Pandit will do what he can. And
your natal chart? Have you brought it with you?"

"I don't carry it around. Ma may still have it somewhere."

The car stops in an upscale bazaar teeming with people and stray dogs. Near the street corner, a rotting refuse pile emits a terrifying stink.

Auntie pays the driver, and we're out, heading toward a storefront reading "Pandit Parsai" in English, followed by several words in Bengali.

Inside, two men sit cross-legged facing each other on the floor. The younger, chubby man jabbers in Hindi, his face animated, arms gesticulating. The other man—tall, gray-haired, and long-nosed—wears a *dhoti punjabi*. His stately demeanor recalls the late prime minister Nehru. He nods and whispers "ha, ha," at regular intervals. *Ha* means "yes" in Hindi. Neither man looks at us.

The air hangs thick with the heady scent of patchouli incense, and a brass statue of the Hindu elephant god, Ganesh, sits just inside the doorway. His great belly protrudes. One of his brass tusks is broken. As the story goes, Ganesh used his broken tusk to write the ancient Vedas, the four ancient texts of Hinduism. Ganesh is known as the Remover of Obstacles, bringer of good luck. Every Vedic astrologer's office has a Ganesh.

Auntie kneels to kiss his feet. I want to turn and run. Instead I follow Auntie's example, then straighten and clasp my hands in front of me. On the bookshelves: the Mahabharata, the Bhagavad-Gita, the Ramayana, and numerous volumes about astrology, healing rituals, and childhood development. In one corner is a devotional altar. I don't recognize the many-armed goddess surrounded by dried lotus flowers, sweets, and snacks. My mouth waters. My fingers itch to grab a *roshogolla*, candy made from milk and sugar, but I don't want to annoy the goddess.

Crammed in next to the altar is a Hewlett-Packard computer on a wooden desk piled with books and paper. A golden elephant screensaver dances across the monitor.

There's no reception area or chairs, so Auntie and I wait awkwardly near the door until the men stand, bow, and press the palms of their hands together in front of their chests, in a gesture of prayer called *namaste,* which means, "The divine light in me salutes the divine light in you."

The chubby man stares at me on his way out, his critical gaze skewering my clothes.

"Come, come, my dear girls." Pandit Parsai gestures toward the carpet. We sit cross-legged in a triangle on the concrete floor. My tailbone will be bruised for days.

Pandit takes Auntie's hands and smiles. "My dearest Kiki, how are your son and daughters? How have you been maintaining your health?" His words flow clear and cool like water.

"My son ran away to his tea gardens, my girls neglect me, and my corns are paining, Pandit." Auntie makes the *namaste* sign and bows her head. I follow suit. I have a kink in my neck.

Pandit does the sideways head nod and clicks his tongue. "You're always in the wrong footwear, Kiki. Have I not told you?"

"Hah, you have." Auntie gazes at her feet, clad in Indian sandals, *kolhapuri chappals*. The corns bulge at the joints of both her big toes.

Pandit turns to gaze at me. I have the uncomfortable feeling he's reaching inside my head and twisting my neurons.

"My dear Lina Ray. Last time I saw you, you were just a baby."

"I'm sorry I don't remember you, Pandit. It's an honor to meet you."

"Quite a fat baby you were. Now you're too thin."

My ears heat up.

Auntie elbows me. "You see, the pandit has a perfect memory."

"Have you brought the natal charts?" He gazes at me with mild expectation.

"I, um, haven't got them. I didn't know I would be seeing you."

He doesn't blink. I wonder if he ever blinks. I wonder if his eyelids even close. Maybe they're perpetually open, on the alert, like gecko eyes. "No matter. Your auntie has given some information, and I've done what I can." He speaks to her in rapid Bengali.

I clear my throat. "Excuse me. What are you saying? I don't understand."

His eyebrows furrow. *"Bangla bolo na?"*

Auntie shakes her head, her cheeks jiggling. "I've tried to teach her—"

"I don't have much opportunity to speak Bengali in San Francisco," I say. "Ma and Baba sometimes spoke in Bengali when we were growing up, but our friends spoke English. Besides, our parents wanted us to assimilate into American culture."

"Such a shame." Pandit Parsai clicks his tongue again. "I'm telling your auntie that your fiancé is problematic."

"Problematic? He's perfect!"

"You must look east."

"I did. I live in the States. India is east from there."

"Your true home is here." He touches my forehead as if checking for a fever. His fingers are cold. "And I see many more problems."

"Oh, Vishnu! What problems?" Auntie groans.

"There's no problem, Mr. Pandit. With all respect, how could you know? You haven't met my fiancé." My fingers curl into fists.

Pandit rubs his nose with his forefinger. "Your fiancé is a cipher, ephemeral. It is as if . . . as if . . ."

"As if what?" I snap.

"As if he does not exist." He takes Auntie's hand. "I'm concerned for this dear girl."

"Oh, Vishnu, oh, Vishnu," Auntie says. "What to do?"

"Nothing!" I shout. "Everything's fine."

Pandit shakes his head. "Kiki, you must go."

"Go where?" Auntie and I reply in unison.

"To America, of course. You must meet the fiancé."

Auntie's mouth drops open. "Me? Go to America?"

"Hah, hah. You must approve the match."

"How will I know, Pandit? Will there be a sign?"

"You'll know." Pandit touches her chest with his forefinger. "In your heart."

Auntie sucks in a long breath. "I'll *know*."

I hold up my hands. "Wait, wait. *I* know him best. Let me decide, okay? He's my fiancé."

Auntie and Pandit give me horrified looks. Auntie straightens her back. "I shall come to America."

"Auntie, you needn't—"

"It's time for a trip abroad, and in any case, your Baba's birthday bash falls in two months. Quite soon after yours."

My birthday is next week. "Look, Auntie, give this some thought—"

She lumbers to her feet. "Say nothing more. It is decided."

Six

San Francisco in late August.

City of cable cars, Beat poets, flower children, Alcatraz. My city of dreams stretches out, vast and uncomplicated. I'm at ease as the plane descends over rolling hillsides dotted with rows of identical rooftops. I take comfort in the familiar curve of the shoreline, the Golden Gate Bridge rising red through the mist. Skyscrapers and highways run straight and symmetrical. The streets are scoured, the sky polished to a shine. Here, I can drink water free of parasites and walk around naked in my apartment. No relatives breathe down my neck, and the doors are made of solid wood with real brass knobs and locks. It's hard to believe the chaotic city of Kolkata even exists.

I take the shuttle to my North Beach apartment, blissfully bright and adorned with hanging plants, books, and hardwood floors. My anchors calm me—reminders that I belong here: messages from friends on my answering machine, a slew of unread e-mails, envelopes stuffed into my mailbox.

I'm home, and here for only two months before Auntie will descend like Godzilla. She'll destroy the city and eat all my friends if I don't find a real fiancé in time. I should spend every minute of every day perusing the personal ads and combing the streets for the elusive Man of My Dreams. Not just for my family, but for myself.

I fall into a jetlag-induced coma, and in the morning, I hop the bus to my office on California Street. Lakshmi, the owner of the agency, works at home, and I rarely see her, but she calls in frequently. I look forward to seeing Donna, office associate and friend.

An hour after I've cleared all the e-mail that has accumulated while I was away, I daydream while listening to a client, Mr. Sen, extol his masculine virtues.

"I am active runner. I enjoy sports, meditation, golf, travel, and gardening. I like the outdoors in general." He resembles a tanned version of Prince Charles in a tight blue suit. I wish he would stop tapping his fingers on the arm of the chair.

"All that? Wow! Impressive. I need you to fill out this personal preferences questionnaire." I glance out the window at cotton clouds dabbing the Bay Bridge.

Mr. Sen leans forward. "I want to settle down with attractive and motivated woman, a professional girl, beautiful inside and out, with similar family background who can complement and enhance my family."

I imagine his dream woman as a curved glass vase in his hallway, complementing and enhancing his family. I think of Raja Prasad, looking for the perfect, docile wife. Like the robot nanny in Ray Bradbury's science fiction story. She always smiles, always loves the children, never grows old. Never has a need of her own, except to be spritzed with WD-40 now and then.

"Of course I'll help, Mr. Sen, but I need to know more about you." I push the forms across the desk.

"My father is a well-reputed family physician. Retired, of course. My grandmother is an intelligent and pious lady."

"Your wife will be lucky to marry into such a family."

"My family prefers a girl of Brahmin roots."

"Of course." I jot down notes. *Stuffy upper crust.*

"I prefer woman nineteen to twenty-fourish, no older." In other words, his own personal flight attendant.

"I'll keep that in mind." Mr. Sen is thirty-three, so why can't he choose a woman his own age? Long ago, I stopped asking this question aloud. Most men who come in here, no matter how old, want young, nubile virgins. Dream on, I want to say. This is the twenty-first century. I grit my teeth and keep silent.

"And fair, very fair complexion preferred." He stares at my dark face, which in Indian personal ads would be classified as "wheatish." "Slim, athletic build. No children. I prefer that she has never been married."

"Of course. I'll find just the right woman for you. What do you do for a living?"

"I am a hardworking professional, building my career in the finance industry."

"Mmm-hmmm." So he's a banker, investment consultant, financial analyst? Why can't he be specific?

He taps the chair, and suddenly I'm aware of the wall clock ticking away the hour. Another client waits in the foyer. I hear Donna chatting on the phone in her office next door.

"—pursuing CFP course," Mr. Sen is saying. "I have master's degree—"

"Your annual income?"

His face reddens. "Fifty thousand to seventy-five thousand."

I think of Ma asking how much money my fiancé makes. If I have to say we split up, I'll say he won the lottery and moved to a Caribbean island. "I don't mean to get too personal, Mr. Sen, but if I'm to find you a good wife, I must know everything."

"I've tried the online dating services. Internet, you know? No luck." He shakes his head. "When will you find?"

"I'll need a little time." I ponder the possibilities. Miss Chatterjee! She was in here last week. Just his type. I stand and extend my hand.

Mr. Sen shakes it. "When shall I have my first date?"

"This week, I promise." I escort him to the reception area, where Mrs. Mukerjee and her demure daughter Sonya are waiting. Sonya's wearing a candy-cotton-pink *churidar kurta*.

Mr. Sen strides past everyone and out the door.

"Ah, lovely Lina!" Mrs. Mukerjee slaps my cheeks and embraces me in a rib-breaking hug. "I must shower you with congratulations!" She steps back and regards me with a teary gaze. "We were all hoping and praying that the gods would send you the right husband, one who would not mind that you are so old, and look, our prayers have been answered. Who is the man? Why the big secret? I'm telling everyone he's a rich Marwari businessman, royalty straight from Rajasthan, but nobody believes me."

"He's not rich Marwari. He's rich . . . Bengali."

"*Acha*. What's his name?"

"Raja," I blurt out. I must have Raja on my mind.

"Ah, Raja. A true king!" Mrs. Mukerjee shrieks.

Just then Kali bursts in, clenching and unclenching her hands. "Lina, I have to talk to you now!"

"If you'll excuse me." I give Mrs. Mukerjee an apologetic look.

In my office, Kali slumps into an armchair, her cleavage nearly spilling from her too-tight paisley dress. "Oh, my knickers are in a twist!"

"About what? Make it quick. I'm working."

"Remember the man I met in India? The one with mojo? Dev? I'm falling for him."

I press the back of my hand to my forehead. "How many times have you seen him?"

"Only once, at Durga's wedding—"

"Oh, Kali! How can you be falling for him?"

"We spoke on the phone. Long distance."

"How many times?"

"Only once, but—"

"Did he say he was falling for you?"

"Well, no, but he was polite. He's also rich. He's studying here, so he'll be back from India soon. He wants to meet."

"Then reserve judgment until you see him again."

"There's something else. His family used to own palaces."

"So?"

"He has an older brother. They're princes. Descended from royalty."

I groan. "Princes marry princesses, Kali. Not the daughters of doctors. Why don't you date someone at work?"

"I don't meet guys at work. How many straight men do

you think work in layout for *City Chic* magazine? Zero. Zilch. Nada."

"You haven't even *dated* this guy."

"I wish you could've met him. His brother is named after a king. Raja."

The blood drains from my face. "What's their surname? Dev and Raja who?"

"Prasad. Dev Prasad and Raja Prasad, princes. I can't believe it."

I grip the edge of my desk. "Princes?"

"Sons of the late Maharajah Ranjit Prasad. Raja and Dev could be the most eligible bachelors in all of India."

How can Raja be a prince? What did I expect? That he would walk around with a crown on his head? How does a prince act, anyway?

"Your fiancé, have you heard from him?" Kali gets up and adjusts her dress, what there is of it.

My face heats up. "As a matter of fact, he's here. He wanted to be back for my birthday." Lies, lies.

"Well. It's about time. What's his name? Come on."

"Raja." I think of Mrs. Mukerjee, waiting to tell the world.

Kali's eyes widen. "Not the same Raja—"

"It's a coincidence. Raja is a common name in India."

As soon as Kali leaves, I pick up the phone, my hand shaking, and call my good friend Harry Kumar. "Harry, I'm in big trouble. I need to talk."

Seven

On my thirtieth birthday, Kali shows up in a low-cut summer dress, saffron yellow this time. In a fog of Calvin Klein perfume, she dumps several packages on the dining table and glances around with a shrewd eye. "Where is he, huh? Mr. Perfect Raja? Hiding in the bedroom? Hello! Mr. Dream Man!" Her heels clack on the hardwood floor as she makes her way to the kitchen.

"Kali, pipe down. He's at work. Had a meeting at . . . Bank of the West."

She narrows her gaze. "Why haven't I seen you dating this guy?"

"Well . . . You, uh, moved to the city only a month ago, didn't you? You wouldn't know him."

She grabs the shiny brown bag of coffee grounds. "Caffeinated Peet's, Major Dickason's Blend. A man after my own heart. Are you going to start drinking coffee now?"

I shake my head. "He's the coffee aficionado. I'm a tea woman." Thank you, Harry, for providing your coffee.

She already has the fridge open. "Aha! I knew it. He drinks real organic whole milk. No more unsweetened soy milk."

"What does it matter what he drinks?"

"Real men don't drink soy. He bought a bottle of chardonnay."

She races out to the living room and grabs Harry's blue Ralph Lauren shirt from the couch. "He's a size Extra Large." She brings the shirt to her nose and inhales. "Smells good, too. Polo cologne?"

"Chanel for Men."

"He has taste. What's this?" She drops the shirt, dashes to the fireplace, and sniffs the two dozen long-stemmed red roses in a crystal vase. "Oh, they smell wonderful. There's a note. *To my one and only rose, on her birthday.* He's so romantic. Beautiful handwriting, too."

"What did you expect?" I clasp my hands in front of me as she opens the closet in the foyer.

"He's a size *thirteen* boot. The man is a giant." She squeals.

"Remember, he's my man, not yours." I trail her into the bedroom. She points at the suitcase on the chair in the corner, then rushes over and grabs a pair of Harry's black Ralph Lauren briefs. "Does he look like the male model on the package?"

"I don't study underwear pictures, Kali."

"Well, I do." She picks up a pair of jeans. "A Tommy Hilfiger man? Oh, Lina."

I snatch the jeans from her, drop them in Harry's suitcase, and slam the lid shut. "That's as far as you go, Miss Nosy."

She goes to the dresser and grabs the shiny black stone, Star Galaxy. I should've hidden it in a drawer.

"What's this? It's beautiful. Where did you get it? Did he give it to you?" She holds the stone up to the light. "Look at the weird white speckles."

"Yes, he gave it to me." I snatch the stone from her and put it on the dressing table. She focuses on the computer beneath the bay window with a view of Coit Tower. It's a clear, true blue San Francisco morning. On a day like this, imaginary men come to life.

She picks up a printed e-mail in blue and pink type. *"Only two days until I hold you in my arms again. . . . "*

I snatch the paper from her. "That's private."

"Why are you keeping him a secret? I won't tell, promise."

"He's nobody you know. I met him at a function for foreign dignitaries . . . a party thrown by a . . . prominent client."

"I'll meet him today, then he won't be a secret anymore."

Harry's belongings will have to do, for now. What will happen when my family realizes Raja won't be here for my birthday party?

At one-thirty, my parents and friends arrive. Ma and Baba drove all the way up from Santa Barbara. They're staying with friends in Berkeley. Ma made *samosas* and *pakoras*. Donna from work and a few others trickle in, and then my best friend Harry Kumar arrives alone. I take his coat, stand on tiptoe to whisper in his ear. "Where's Jonathan?"

"I figured your family wasn't ready for him yet." He winks, stunning in Ralph Lauren shirt and form-fitting jeans.

"You could pretend to be just friends," I say, disappointed. I like Jonathan. I was the one who set up the two of them on their first blind date.

"I don't pretend, Lina. I'm not comfortable giving you all my stuff—"

"It's just for a while. You're not actually *impersonating* my fiancé," I whisper.

"Then who will?"

"I'll find someone." I kiss his cheek, inhale his cologne. I've often fantasized about him, but where will that lead? He could be a movie star in Bollywood, India's equivalent of Hollywood. He once auditioned in Mumbai—formerly Bombay—but nobody would hire him because his Hindi accent was too Americanized. He became a commercial airline pilot instead.

We congregate in the living room, where Ma lights a single candle on the chocolate cake. I make a wish, blow out the candle, and we feast on the snacks. The afternoon passes in a soft rhythm of friends and family, until Baba proclaims in a loud voice, "Where is this Raja? Why is he not here?"

"He'll be home shortly." I throw Harry a *help me* look.

"He's practically moved in," Kali says in a low voice.

Harry ducks out to the liquor store, and a few minutes later, the telephone rings.

"That's him!" Kali shrieks, scrambling for the wall phone in the kitchen. Her face goes gaga as she says, "Hello, yes, lovely to talk to you, we've heard so much about you." Then she covers the mouthpiece and shouts, "He's got an emergency at work! Can't come now."

Baba shakes his head. Ma's lips turn down in disappointment. My heartbeat picks up as I rush to the phone.

"He has an utterly cool voice." Kali hands me the phone, her hand still over the mouthpiece. She runs back to the living room. I hear her talking to the family. *It's him. You should hear his voice. Deep baritone. God, he sounds fantastic . . .*

"Hello, Raja?" I say tentatively into the telephone.

"Lina." Harry's voice reverts to normal, which is still deep and smooth. "You have to do something about this problem."

Eight

$\mathcal{I}$ dream of my deceased fiancé, Nathu. He strides toward me in his khaki pants and windbreaker, his shoulders hunched against the cold. We're visiting the Japanese Garden in Golden Gate Park. I run into his arms, relish his particular scents of cloves and citrus. He loved mandarin oranges.

I was sure he was dead, but here he is in the flesh, the gentle man who wouldn't kill a spider. He put bugs outside, where they smashed into car windshields instead.

"Why did you make us have a memorial service for you?" I ask as we walk hand in hand.

"I tried to tell everyone I wasn't really gone. Nobody listened."

"But the accident on Highway One. You spun out near Mendocino. They found your car mangled at the bottom of a cliff!"

He shrugs. "Yeah, it was me, but there was a mix-up. I didn't really die."

"I canceled the engagement. That was two years ago. You left me to clean up the mess, like I was in a Lifetime movie that played over and over—"

"I'm sorry, Lina. I tried to contact you."

"We were all so sad. What you put us through. Your mother returned to India for the funeral rituals. You were cremated. I'm sorry I didn't go. I couldn't. I was too broken up."

"It's okay. It was all a mistake. I'm back, and I want you to find a man."

I let go of his hand. "What about you? You're here."

"You need to move on." He bends down, picks a beetle off the sidewalk, and pops it into his mouth. He crunches, the sound grating my eardrums.

Horror hits me. "You're not Nathu. He really *is* dead, isn't he? This is a trick."

I wake up clutching the bedcovers.

Nine

The next morning I look for Harry at the Treehouse Cafe not far from my apartment. Brooding ocean fog blocks out the sunshine.

I weave through the crowd of nose-ringed, black-haired students hunched over round tables. Here and there, a shimmering thread connects two lovers, their gazes locked in love. A memory touches my heart—Nathu grabbing my hand, holding my palm to his cheek. The ghostlike thread between us always trembled, as if it knew Nathu would die.

"Lina, over here!" Harry waves, stretching his long, jeans-clad legs under the table. He's hip and masculine in a black turtleneck. If he weren't so handsome, he'd be pretty.

I order my usual Earl Grey and bring the steaming cup to the table. I sit across from him.

"So, My Love." He vocally places capital letters on the words. He grips my fingers and gives the back of my hand a soft kiss. "Where shall we marry? India or here? I could fly us to Maui."

I pull my hand away. "I know I've got myself into deep dog doo—"

"Deeper than dog doo. Elephant doo." He sips his usual double-tall mocha with whipped cream.

"Okay, Ganesh doo. I appreciate everything you're doing for me. I really do."

"My love poetry is improving, don't you think?"

"That last poem was Emily Dickinson."

"Hey, you needed a fiancé. Don't complain."

"I'm not. I'm thanking you."

"You're welcome, but why keep lying?"

"I'm not." I run a finger along the rim of my teacup. "I'm stretching the truth like a rubber band."

"Pretty convenient having a fake fiancé to boss around." He takes a long sip of his mocha. A ray of sunlight breaks through the fog, reflecting off his hair. I never noticed the red highlights.

"If I don't, my aunt might send Pee-wee to America."

"Why don't you marry him?"

I screw up my nose, as if I actually smell the elephant doo. "He has yellow, crooked teeth and a squeaky voice. He practically drooled on me."

Harry shrugs. "Maybe he's a nice guy. You didn't give him a chance—"

"Would *you* sleep with Pee-wee?"

He grins. "Well, depends on how big his—"

"Spare me the details."

"You have to stand up to your parents. Tell them to back off."

"My great-aunt will be here to meet Raja. This astrologer, Pandit Parsai, predicted problems. He said my fiancé was *ephemeral.*"

"Knows what he's talking about, this pandit."

"I'm letting my parents down by not getting married and having kids. My father gets indigestion. Ma dreams of a grand wedding with all our family and friends in attendance. In India, everyone knows everything about everyone else. It's a big soap opera."

"You live here. Do whatever you want."

"I feel a connection with my family, Harry. I love them. I want them to be happy, and I want to be happy too. But the two things seem to be mutually exclusive."

"You do what you need to do for yourself. Your family will come around."

"Nothing will please them. My father wanted a son. I was his firstborn, a girl. We're all girls!"

"You gotta get a grip. This is about Nathu, isn't it?"

"Not again." I lean back and roll my eyes toward the ceiling. I say nothing about the dream. I have crazy nightmares all the time. They don't mean much.

"You don't want to talk about him, but he rules you. A dead guy."

A dead guy. I want to believe Nathu faked the car accident to escape and start a new life. He's relaxing on a tropical island, sipping piña coladas and digging his toes into the warm sand. "Nobody rules me. I direct my own life."

"Come on, Lina. You can't lie to me. How long have I known you?"

Since we were both freshmen at Santa Barbara High School, when Harry still conducted his love life in the closet. "Too long."

"You're scared. I see it in your eyes."

I gulp my tea and say nothing. "Must be a reflection of your own eyes."

He leans forward and takes my hands, more tenderly this time. A new, slim gold band glints on the third finger of his left hand. "Honey, not every guy is going to drive off a cliff, okay? It was a freak accident."

My mouth goes dry, and I hate myself for letting the past ambush me. "Oh, Harry. Why couldn't you have been straight?"

"I was born crooked, baby."

To my surprise, I find myself close to tears. "Nathu was perfect. He didn't even leave the toilet seat up."

"You're romanticizing him. Remember the nights he'd forget to check in, and you'd call me to talk because you were worried? Remember the way he used to drive, even with you in the car? He had a death wish, and he was willing to drag you into the afterlife, too."

A tear trickles down my cheek. "He did like to take risks."

"You loved him, but was it Nathu you loved, or your idea of Nathu? You thought he might be seeing someone else."

My stomach squeezes. "There was nobody else." Leave me to my imagination, I'm thinking. Let me believe Nathu was who I wanted him to be.

"He forgot to call late at night, showed up in the same wrinkled clothes he wore the day before. You know the truth, and it hurts. That's why you won't give anyone else a chance."

"Ouch." Harry has always been blunt, but that's what I love about him. "What am I going to do?"

"Try widening your net. Nobody will ever live up to your expectations."

"You do, Harry, but you're taken." I look around the room, as if my imaginary man sits nearby in disguise. "I know I need to get out more, but every good-looking guy has some neurosis or narcissistic complex. Every nice guy is either married or looks like a variation on Pee-wee Herman or Danny DeVito."

"Danny DeVito isn't bad-looking." Harry finishes his coffee and stands up. "I can't help you much longer. Jonny and I are planning a commitment ceremony in two weeks. You're my maid of honor."

I'm stunned. Two weeks? Commitment ceremony? I'll be the Old Maid of Honor.

"Congratulations," I manage to say. I scramble to my feet. "I'm so happy for you. Are you sure he's the right one?"

"He leaves his underwear lying around, but we love each other."

"Wonderful news." My smile hides a nagging emptiness.

"Thank you for setting us up. You have a sixth sense about these things." Harry speaks in a blithe, buoyant tone, which makes me feel even more bereft.

"It's all in the math." My mouth is dry.

"After the ceremony we're moving to Paris. I'll be based there on Air France."

Harry's words fall on my feet with a thud. "You're what? You're leaving?"

"We'll ship our furniture by sea. We'll only have suitcases. We'll also have to give up our apartment a few days early. If it's not too much of an imposition, could we stay with you?"

"Of course. I'll sleep on the couch."

"Oh, in that case we'll stay in a hotel—"

"I won't hear of it."

"Thanks a million. Look, honey. Come visit us in Paris. Flights are cheap now."

"Harry—" *You can't leave me.* "What will I do?"

He shrugs. "Find a fiancé, or don't. It's a free country."

I stand and watch him stride out, all heads turning to watch his smooth gait. He's a model on a runway, and here I am, invisible. I've spent my life being happy for other people. Joining their hands, helping them on the road to their shared futures, while my future slips into the ditch.

Ten

The day passes in a haze. I see three new clients, one a millionaire land developer who wants a perfect blond to drape over his arm; Mrs. Mukerjee calls to say Sonya liked her last date, but the man wants a younger woman. He'll have to date an embryo.

All afternoon I field calls, enter data, and find myself staring more than once at a blank computer screen.

Around four o'clock, a call comes in. Nothing but static. Probably a Japanese golf company CEO looking for a voluptuous American wife. A distant voice shouts *Hello, Hello*. He can't hear my reply, so I hang up.

ANJALI BANERJEE

When I have a few minutes to breathe, I spread out files and photographs of male clients, and then Donna walks right in, drops an envelope in my in-box, and sits across from me. She has the pale skin of a vampire and the porcelain features of a Nordic queen. She's divorced and has a five-year-old boy in kindergarten.

I open the envelope. Mr. Sen enclosed photos of himself walking past the Palace of Fine Arts, posing in front of the Wax Museum at Fisherman's Wharf, sitting cross-legged on a black couch in a stark living room. In each shot, he looks like a paper cutout pasted onto the background.

I sense his loneliness. He would rather be in India, surrounded by his mother, his four sisters and two brothers. Here in America, he's a prop without a past.

Donna's delicately penciled eyebrows furrow. "What's going on? What are you doing with those photos?"

"Research."

"What kind of research?" She picks up a postcard from the windowsill.

I spin around and snatch the card from her. The image is an old black-and-white shot of a double-decker Paris accumulator tram, with "Philippe du Roule Vanves" written on the side and the Eiffel Tower in the background. I read Harry's handwriting. *My dearest Lina, Loving Paris, but there's an ache in my heart. I wish you were here. With love and affection, xoxoxoxoxo.*

72

"The man's trilingual, and he never includes a signature," Donna says. She doesn't notice that the postmark stamp is from Daly City instead of Paris. Any moment, the jig will be up, and I'm tired of letting the lies accumulate behind my eyes.

"If I tell you something, will you promise to keep it a secret? You'll understand, but my family won't. I've dug myself into a deep pit."

"What is it?"

I take a deep breath. "I don't really have a fiancé."

"What?"

I tell her the story, and she breaks into easy laughter. "You're something else, woman."

I feel marginally better, now that I've told her.

"I need to find a real guy before Auntie Kiki arrives." I put the postcard next to the others. The Taj Mahal, a big stone face sculpture in Paris, an aerial shot of Amsterdam.

Donna riffles through the photos. "I'll help with your research. I'm an expert. Here, this guy's an intern at S. F. General. Perfect guy."

The picture shows a handsome Indian man with a full head of hair, average eyes, and an average smile. Fair-skinned to wheatish. A surgeon-in-training. A man my parents will adore.

"I shouldn't date a client," I say.

Donna purses her lips. "My job is to find the perfect

73

ANJALI BANERJEE

mate for my clients. Now you're my client, okay?"

"Could be a conflict of interest." I roll my chair back and cross my arms over my chest. "I don't usually date Indian men coming straight from the mother country."

"There's always a first time."

"They expect their wives to starch their shirts."

"Send them to the dry cleaners." Donna peruses his profile. "He's looking for a professional woman. Age, caste, and religious affiliation don't matter."

"What if I'm a Jehovah's Witness?"

"You're not." Donna waves another photograph in front of my face. "How about this guy? He's here on scholarship."

The photo shows an Andre Agassi lookalike lobbing a tennis ball over a net. "No athletes," I say.

"What, you have a problem with rippling triceps?"

"I'll see the surgeon, Mr.——"

"Dutta. Dilip Dutta."

After Donna leaves, I open my desk drawer and pull out Nathu's portrait, still in the teak frame his mother gave me. I run my fingers along the glass. Nathu, face to the wind, sitting on a rock in Yosemite National Park, the sunlight reflecting off his perfect teeth. A handsome man, chiseled features—fair-skinned and a touch effeminate. Was he seeing other women?

Maybe this charade is for the best. I'll meet a new Knight

in Shining Armor. I think of what Harry said. *Try widening your net.* Okay, so the man's armor doesn't have to shine. It could be rusty.

I hope I'm not heading for doom on this date with Dr. Dilip.

Eleven

$\mathcal{I}$ need something to wear.

I've come to the mall with Kali. She wants me to buy a skintight dress ten sizes too small.

Teenagers breeze by in their navel-baring shirts and retro bell-bottoms, rings through their noses. Kali drags me into Victoria's Secret. The store buzzes with customers—some couples, some single men. Pheromone-soaked perfume fills the air. I'm surrounded by transparent, X-rated intimates, black panties, satin push-up bras, and not-there nightgowns. A bright, shimmering thread vibrates between the store clerk and a man perusing the underwear. I consider rushing over to introduce the two lovebirds, but they're already gawking at each other.

As Kali sifts through the lace panties, my mind wanders to Raja Prasad. India seems so distant now, a mirage, yet he sneaks into my memory. I think of the three forms of twilight and imagine him gazing at the stars. I wonder whether he always gives stones to women. He's probably found a perfect, obedient wife. I wonder whether she wears skimpy lingerie. I wonder—

"Here, this'll look smashing on you." Kali holds up a black thong, a strip of floss attached to a waistband.

"Too risqué for a date with a doctor."

"He probably sees naked women at work every day," Kali says. "Is he a gynecologist?"

A couple of heads turn our way.

"Keep your voice down!" I whisper. "No, he's not, and I'm not stripping for him."

"Oh, behave! You have no guts. How about this?" She grabs a red lace teddy. "Here, perfect!"

"Do you wear this stuff, Kali? Do Ma and Baba know?"

"Of course they don't know. They would both have heart attacks." She pulls me to the mirror. "Raja will be so *switched on*."

"Look, Kali—" Why did I choose the name, Raja? Freudian slip? If I tell Kali I'm making up the fiancé, what will she think? I have to tell her. The truth dances on my lips, then she says, "You know, Baba hasn't been well again."

I swallow my words. "What's happened?"

"Another bout of the flu, probably from one of his patients. He works too hard, and then Ma starts to complain of this or that ache. They're both such wrecks. I worry." She picks a set of pink lace underpants and bra for herself.

"I worry too." If I tell the truth now, our parents will end up in the ER. Or worse.

Twelve

I yank all the clothes from my closet and throw everything on the bed. Ten different pairs of baggy pajamas. I love pajamas. I'd wear them to work, shopping, to nightclubs, if I could. I own only a few dresses. They fit my curves two years ago, but now I'm verging on anorexic.

You're beautiful, my imaginary man says from the chair in the corner. He's in khaki slacks and a denim shirt with the two top buttons undone. He watches me peel off my blazer, blouse, and pants.

I try on the sleeveless purple dress I wore for Nathu. I look like a dehydrated grape. Then I try on a black tube dress, which makes me resemble a burned breakfast sausage.

All those clothes look sexy on you, my imaginary man says. *But I prefer you in nothing at all.* I picture him lighting a cloves cigarette. Nathu smoked but didn't live long enough to let it kill him. He inhales, then sends the smoke curling up to the ceiling.

"I can't go to dinner in nothing," I mutter, heading for the bathroom to shower.

Why go at all? He follows me, slips out of his clothes, and joins me in the shower.

"I have to get out of this apartment once in a while." I grab sandalwood soap and work up lather.

Why not stay home? We'll put on a little music. Barry White. Open a bottle of champagne.

Barry White? I prefer Dave Matthews.

I wash quickly, rinse, and jump out of the shower. "I can't stay. I have to find someone my parents will like. Someone with whom I can settle down. A guy who makes money, from a good family—"

I come from a good family. I make oodles of money.

"It's not real money. It's like . . . Monopoly money! You're a Monopoly game guy."

I picture him shrugging as he watches me choose a conservative maroon dress.

So what? I can satisfy you. What's wrong with me?

"Nothing." I brush my hair, apply a shade of lipstick to match my dress. "You're perfect, except you're not real."

I'm as real as this bed. He pats the mattress, comes toward me, and kisses the back of my neck. His lips whisper across my skin.

Stay. Climb into bed with me.

"And do what? Have imaginary sex?" I press my fingers to my temples. "Oh, I'm talking to myself. My neighbors will hear. They'll know I've lost my mind."

Who cares what they think? He lies on the bed. Naked.

I turn away, force myself to finish getting ready. Then I leave him in the apartment and lock the door.

Thirteen

$\mathcal{D}$r. Dilip Dutta wears his white shirt buttoned to the top, a red tie strangling his thin neck. His calm features remind me of the Buddha. His steady fingers rearrange his knife and fork on either side of the plate. He sips ice water, then puts the glass down at the top right corner of the plate.

"You look lovely," he says in the congenial voice of a yoga instructor.

"Thank you—I didn't have a thing to wear." I twist my right earring. Greens Restaurant is crowded on Sunday evening, the conversation a steady background buzz of white noise and clinking dinnerware. The dramatic views of Alcatraz, the Golden Gate Bridge, and the Marin Headlands mesmerize me. I imagine flying out across the water, alighting on a sailboat, and floating away into solitude.

"Your haircut is avant-garde. I like the modern look." Dr. Dutta pats his own hair, combed to a fault.

Modern as opposed to what, antique? "Yours is unusual too. Very . . . smooth."

"I have to keep it short for work." His smile reveals straight, yellowed teeth. I wonder if he smokes. Doctors know the health hazards of smoking, don't they? Maybe he drinks too much coffee. Or maybe he had a high fever as a child or had acne and took antibiotics. I hear tetracycline leaves stains on your teeth. Oh, I'm thinking about teeth.

"Short hair is good." I nod, keep nodding like a bobbleheaded doll, then sip my water.

He unfolds the cloth napkin and flattens the corners. Then he opens the menu, carefully running his finger past each item.

I pretend to read the list of specials while regarding him. If he were my surgeon, I'd trust him. His hands wouldn't slip. He wouldn't make a mistake or forget a detail. He would arrange the options and weigh each one. He'll be well regarded in his profession. Patients will flock to him from all over the world. He has a trustworthy face—a doctor's caring, bland features and the Buddha's serene gaze.

I refocus on the menu. "So much green stuff. Makes me feel like a rabbit."

"That's the name of the restaurant. Greens. If you'd like to go somewhere else, we can—"

"No, no, this is fine. I like leaves and dandelions." I sound lame, but Dr. Dilip Dutta doesn't inspire me to poetry. His meticulousness makes me want to run home and mess up my apartment, toss my paper clips like confetti.

He points to the appetizers. "The Thai spiced potato cake with wasabi looks good."

"I'm not a big wasabi fan. How about the marinated feta, asparagus, and melon salad?"

His nose crinkles. "I'm allergic to cheese."

"Then we'll skip the appetizer." I try not to sound irritated. These stockings scratch my legs. I never wear stockings. Why am I wearing them tonight? I feel like a bachelorette on *The Dating Game*.

I glance at the couple sitting to our right. They lean over the table toward each other, their words slicing the space between them. They're fighting. At least they're discussing something dramatic.

"I'll try the fresh pea ravioli with snap, snow, and English peas," Dilip says, pronouncing each word as if it stands on its own.

"Then I'll have the linguini with caramelized onions and gorgonzola cream."

"A woman of taste." He closes the menu and signals the waiter.

After we order, Dilip gives me an assessing look, elbows on the table. An awkward silence follows, then the waiter returns with our drinks. Dilip pours ale into an empty mug, not spilling a drop, then sips and puts down the mug directly opposite his water glass.

I touch my earring again. "So, you're a doctor. What's your specialty?"

"I'm still doing my residency. I'm on Emergency Medicine rotation." I notice a red tinge in the whites of his eyes. I wonder how much sleep he gets.

"That must be exciting. Lots of drama. Do you get many gunshot and stab wounds?"

"A fair amount. We also get sliced fingers and sick babies." He takes another sip of ale.

"I thought I wanted to be a doctor when I was five. I had a doctor's kit, tried it out on imaginary patients."

"Most children play doctor, but few go on to study medicine. Your father's a doctor. Are there any physicians on your mother's side?"

I sense Auntie watching me from afar, analyzing Dr. Dutta. She'd like his reserve, his dedication to his noble profession. He has a certain simplicity, or maybe he has unseen layers, like an onion. Or perhaps he just *smells* like an onion. I'm not close enough to tell whether the smell comes from him or the kitchen.

"They're scientists and engineers. My mother's family

ANJALI BANERJEE

mainly lives in Kolkata, yes, but some have moved to Banga-
lore."

"Ah, the Silicon Valley of India. They're part of the out-
sourcing revolution?"

"I think they like the weather there." I fidget in my chair.
He asks polite questions, but what does it all matter?

"What's your favorite color?" His eyes grow redder by the
minute. The poor man. He probably hasn't slept in a month.

"Maroon. And yours?"

"I'm a fan of cool green. Or maybe it's because I wear
scrubs at work." His eyelids droop.

Then behind him, my imaginary man appears. I try to
blink him away, but the image won't leave. He taps the top of
Dilip's head and gives me a wicked grin. *I told you you
should've stayed home.*

"Don't rub it in." I finish off my wine. Dr. Dutta came to
see me, and he could've been catching up on his shut-eye.

"Excuse me?" Dilip asks, yawning.

"I'm just wondering where our food is."

On cue, the waiter hurries over with a tray. I'm grateful for
the distraction. I try to ignore my fantasy man. At least he
put on some clothes.

The room grows fuzzy. Don't I know not to drink on an
empty stomach?

Dilip finishes his ale, we polish off our meals, and then he
droops forward over his empty plate, his chin lolling against

86

his chest. He quickly straightens and blushes. "Please forgive me." He gathers his cloth napkin and wipes his mouth.

"If you need to go and get some sleep, I won't be offended." A lump of dessert sticks in my throat.

"It's not you. The hospital puts me on one rotation after another. You must work hard too."

"I have to keep names and faces straight in my head, and—"

He's nodded off again, poor guy. He's nice enough, works hard, makes time for a date although he's exhausted. I see no shimmering thread between us, but sometimes the connection needs time to grow. I ought to give him a chance. So why is my heart curled up in the fetal position? All I want to do is sleep.

Fourteen

$\mathcal{M}$y time is short, and Mr. Right remains elusive.

Friday night, I'm on a date with Patrick Malloy, a software gazillionaire who pokes his elbow into me at the Dave Matthews concert at the coliseum. We're in the highest balcony, to the side. The seats press close together. We're all sitting half on top of one another, and Patrick's armpits give off a pungent odor. I lean away, but he angles his elbow to fill the space. He lifts a pair of binoculars to his eyes and sings along to "So Damn Lucky," one of my favorite Dave Matthews songs.

I fantasize about Dave. He's singing to me, only me. The

rest of the audience falls away. He whisks me off in his limo, and we fly to the exotic island of Mykonos.

Maybe I should've returned Dilip's calls. He left two apologetic messages, and I could tell he was calling from the ER both times. Voices echoed on the intercom in the background.

After my date with him, I had a disturbing dream. I was sitting across from Dilip at the restaurant. He slept, chin on his chest. When he looked up again, he wasn't Dilip. He was Raja Prasad, brooding and black as a monsoon. I was supposed to marry him and take care of his mother, but I forgot.

"I do not tolerate insubordination," he said in a deep, menacing voice, and then I woke up.

Now I focus on the guitar threads. Is this the man for me? Mr. Patrick Malloy, Irish-born computer genius extraordinaire? Do I love sideburns, ruddy complexion, and hands the size of baseball mitts? I prefer the image of Dave Matthews serenading me as he sings "Gravedigger" a cappella.

Patrick thrusts the binoculars at me, the damp residue of sweat still on the eyepiece. I wish he would disappear so I can enjoy the concert alone.

I focus the lens on Dave's expressive face. He sings three encores, then Patrick drives me home and I have to dash from the car to escape his sweaty grip. Once inside, I bolt my front door and lean against it, breathing hard. I've just escaped certain death.

My fantasy man breathes down my neck.

You're worse off now than when you started dating. He trails me into the bedroom.

"I'm peachy keen."

See, if you had stayed home—

"What's the secret to finding the perfect man? Maybe I'll never find that special spark with anyone. I'm a matchmaker. I'm not supposed to be the one matched."

You're matched with me.

"I know, that's the problem. I can't enjoy dates. You get in the way." I kick off my high-heeled shoes and hurl them at the image of Nathu. He dissipates as the shoes smack the wall and bounce to the ground.

Then he returns, all patience and caring. *Now, now.*

"Don't you get angry about anything?" I peel off my stockings and massage my sore feet. "I'm not wearing those things again."

You don't have to wear them for me.

I yank off my clothes and pull on flannel pajamas and slippers. "You weren't supposed to follow me. I'm not supposed to think of you when I'm with someone else."

I'm always with you.

I snap my fingers. "Go away."

I'm in your head, in your heart.

"You're a fantasy." Tears push at the back of my throat. I get into bed and pull the covers up to my chin.

I'm real, my love. The words slink through me, warming me to my toes. I feel him beside me, sense his breath, his weight, but he dwells only in my imagination. In the window, there is only a reflection of myself against the night. Alone.

There's no man here, but when I fall asleep, I dream of him. His molecules leave my brain and coalesce. The buzz of electrons and protons spin in space as he becomes flesh and bone, a man with solid arms, torso, legs, hot blood racing through his veins. He slides into bed beside me. I feel his strong heartbeat, his pulse as he kisses me and draws me into a world of pleasure.

Fifteen

Sunday afternoon, I meet the tennis player, Pramit Lall, for a drink at the famous Vesuvio Café, a historical monument to jazz, poetry, and creative Bohemians. The dim saloon, once a hangout for Jack Kerouac, now fills with tourists, executives in pressed suits, and chess players hunching over intense games. The walls are covered with paintings, artwork, and articles from the Beat era.

I find Pramit upstairs at a dim corner table. He's hairier than I expected, but that's okay. No problem, even if the hair emerges from deep inside his nose. I sit across from him, and we make our boring introductions. He orders a

Jack Kerouac—rum, tequila, orange juice, and lime served in a bucket glass—and I order a glass of chardonnay. Then he slips into intimate conversation before I can raise my shield.

"I believe in monogamy." He takes a gulp of his Kerouac. "I believe in focusing on one woman." He gazes at me with bright blue eyes. Does he wear colored contact lenses?

"One woman, like which woman?" I sip my chardonnay, chilled and sweet.

"You. I believe in giving the woman all the attention she needs, whenever she demands it."

"You don't, think . . . um, that a woman should take care of a man?"

"Only if it makes her happy. Whatever she prefers, I prefer. I'm not a man who expects his wife to commit *sati* if he dies. Imagine—the wife burning herself on her husband's funeral pyre. Such practices are barbaric." He touches my cheek. Calluses roughen the palm of his hand, probably from holding his tennis racquet. I hope.

"*Sati* has been outlawed in India," I say.

"Hah, but many women still immolate themselves rather than face life as widows—"

"They should have more options," I say, growing annoyed. "Or they could remarry. My family is Brahmo Samaj, a tradition that has always condemned *sati*."

"Then we're kindred spirits, Ms. Ray."

Come on, you're not that gullible, my imaginary man whispers in my ear. I swat him away.

Pramit waves a hand through the air. "Is there a fly in here? We could move to Molinari's delicatessen."

"That's okay."

He only wants to get into your pants.

"He's a perfect gentleman!" I snap.

"Who is?" Pramit blinks.

"You, of course. You haven't asked about my family or caste."

"All that matters is that you're you."

All that matters is that you're a woman, my phantom says. *You have the correct plumbing.*

Pramit smiles, revealing perfect white teeth, which have probably received thousands of dollars worth of dental work. He reaches across the table and touches my chin in a playful way. I can't stop staring into his eyes, but a nagging voice tells me I'm a moth heading for a headlight.

"We'll see a movie this afternoon," Pramit says. "How would you like that?"

Where he can cop a feel.

I grit my teeth. "I'd love that!"

"How about a classic at the Retro? *Casablanca*?"

"Sounds wonderful."

Pramit puts his muscular, hairy hand over mine, and then I notice the faint band of untanned skin on the third finger of his left hand.

Don't jump to conclusions, I tell myself. You're always eager for a quick way out. Don't sabotage this chance.

Follow your intuition, my imaginary man says behind me.

"What would your wife say?" I ask. Where did that come from? I watch Pramit's eyes to gauge his reaction.

"I'm divorced." He doesn't blink.

See, that wasn't so bad. Divorce isn't the end of the world. Many men are divorced.

"How long were you married?"

"Five years. We were young. It didn't work out."

Ask him about the kids—

"Do you have any children?"

"One son. He's four."

"You didn't mention this on your profile form. There's a spot to check for 'divorced,' 'never married,' or—"

"I didn't want my marital status to hurt my chances with a woman like you." He's smooth as melting toffee.

"You have a child."

"I didn't lie. I simply failed to check the correct box."

"You didn't check any box. A lie of omission is still a lie." My voice rises. What am I doing? This man hasn't done anything wrong. One out of two marriages ends in divorce in this country, and he's allowed to have a son.

Indians don't divorce so easily. Use your brain.

"I bet you aren't divorced." My voice shakes. "In fact, you and your wife probably don't even live apart."

For the first time, Pramit loses his cool. His cheeks redden, and then the smooth look snaps back over his face like blinds. "My wife, you know, she has trouble getting along alone."

"Cut the crap. Thanks for the drink." I stand, crumple my napkin, and throw it on the table.

"Wait a minute, where are you going?"

I grab my coat and purse and stalk out, my imaginary man in tow.

Sixteen

I drive to Ghirardelli Square near Fisherman's Wharf. What better place to lose myself in the crowds? When I get out of the car, my knees wobble.

I've upset you, my imaginary man says.

Oh, no, he's still with me.

"I'm not upset." I stop on the corner, press the Walk buzzer, and watch the tourists. Silvery threads vibrate in the air, linking lovers as they hurry across the street.

There's no thread between anyone and me.

The last thing I want to do is make you angry.

Right! And I might turn into the Incredible Hulk. "I

should thank you, I suppose." The Walk light blinks. I cross the street, not looking to either side. I step up on the curb, nearly stumbling, and head for the safety and warmth of the stores in Ghirardelli.

My imaginary man is still with me. "Get out of here," I tell him. "This is too weird."

Why won't you look at me?

I shake my head, hurry up the steps to the first level. I feel dizzy. I sit on the concrete edge of a fountain. Droplets of cool spray hit the back of my head.

He sits beside me.

My heart aches for the past, for Nathu. This mirage man is Nathu and not Nathu, the past and not the past. My longings, dreams, desires.

"You weren't faithful, were you, Nathu?"

No reply.

"You don't know the answer because you're just some facsimile I created to keep me company. I know this is true now. You weren't perfect at all."

I jump to my feet and run into the Potter's Wheel. He comes after me and whispers. *You're scared to move on. I'm sorry I did this to you.*

I pick up a terra-cotta elephant and turn it over. The sales clerk glares at me over thick glasses slipping down her nose. "Can I help you?"

"No, everything's peachy, thanks." I put the elephant on

the counter and run outside, past the stores and down the steps to the street.

So, I'm imagining a man. Who cares? This time, he saved me from certain heartache with a real jerk. When would I have found out about Pramit? After we'd slept together?

I look up at the stars, except there are no stars. The cloudy sky, reflecting diffused, orange city lights, spits raindrops. I pull my fleece collar up around my neck, hunch into my coat. Desperation unfolds inside me. I'll never give up the past, never be at peace. What am I scared of, really? That there is no perfect man? So what? I could be happy alone, forever.

I hurry back to my car and drive home.

In my apartment, I lock the door and pull both chains across. A sharp pain begins in the back of my head and travels around to my temples. There's no aspirin in the medicine cabinet, so I search the drawers. Cough drops, small travel bottles of lotion, but no aspirin.

I never realized how much junk I've accumulated beneath the illusion of neatness—herbal shampoo bottles, toothbrushes, razors, remnants of sandalwood soap. The kitchen drawers burst with receipts, rubber bands, maps, newspaper articles about travel to exotic countries. *Travel.* I pull out a brochure and stare at the Taj Mahal, the white sand beaches of Goa. My heart aches with longing. My feet itch to roam the world. I think of what the astrologer wrote in my natal chart many years ago. I'll search for love across many seas.

Then I shove the brochure in the garbage.

I switch on the computer and check my e-mail. Several messages from friends and relatives, many congratulating me on my pending marriage, and one from Harry, DREAM-FIANCE54, asking how my date went with Pramit. The headache worsens. I reply, "Peachy. He's married," and shut down the computer.

I check the answering machine. A message from Harry, reminding me about his commitment ceremony at Point Reyes National Seashore. In case I forget to check e-mail. Another blank message, a hang-up.

I'm in the kitchen making tea when the phone rings again. Who could be calling so late? I pick up. "Speak!"

"Hello? Lina Ray?" The voice sounds familiar, but I can't place it.

"Yes, this is Lina."

"Raja Prasad here. Do you remember me?"

My heart flips. "Of course. Mr. Prasad. How are you?" I draw a sharp breath. Across thousands of miles, his voice has the power to send a thrill through me.

"I'm well, thanks. And you?"

"Fine, fine." *Hunky dory, nothing to complain about.* "How did you get my number?" Did he talk to my father? If he did, then he knows about my engagement.

"You told me the name of your company. Lakshmi Matchmakers. I called and spoke to a . . . Donna? I hope you do not consider me too forward."

"Not at all. What can I do for you?" I put on my business-like voice. I won't get personal with the poster boy for chauvinism. Even if he did give me a stone called Star Galaxy.

"I may be in need of your services."

"My . . . services?" All sorts of weird thoughts flash through my mind.

All I hear is "brother," and "right away." Then the line goes dead.

Seventeen

"What a pleasant surprise, Mr. Prasad," I say the next morning at the office. What a complete shock. I want to run into the closet and let out a primal scream, except the closet is cluttered with office supplies. The word *prince* parades through my mind on a royal elephant. What will I say to him? I'll stutter like a fool.

"Call me Raja." Raja Prasad folds into the chair across from my desk. The collar of his white cotton shirt opens at the neck, revealing hints of muscular chest. A custom-tailored black suit falls in a perfect fit.

I saw him once, in semi-darkness. Now, in daylight, he no

longer resembles Krishna, the playful deity. Raja Prasad is rough-edged, like the action-movie hero Vin Diesel, except with hair. The scar on his cheek forms a faint line, a reminder of a violent moment.

He's a prince, a real prince. My fingers tremble holding the pencil. "What can I do for you, Mr. . . . Raja? What brings you to San Francisco?"

"You." He stares, and I turn into a puddle of butter.

"Me?" I point at myself, then regain my bearings. Okay, breathe. You're in your office, on your own turf here.

"You're difficult to recognize in Western clothes." He raises an eyebrow.

I smile. "I wear saris only on special occasions, like at weddings."

"Saris suit you."

Oh, gag me. Does he mean that I look like a bum in my pressed Charter Club slacks and sweater? I fought with my hair this morning. Instead of following orders, it's wreaking havoc in frizzy rebellion. What right does he have to comment on my appearance, anyway? He barged into my office as if he owns the world instead of a few measly palaces. "I'm sorry I couldn't hear everything you said on the phone."

"I apologize for the bad connection. I was flying from Japan." His gaze travels at leisure across the bookshelves, the plants, the paperwork on my desk, and lingers on the postcards from Harry. I'm thankful that the writing faces the wall.

He fixes his spotlight gaze on me again. "And how are your parents? Your auntie? Your sisters?"

"They're all peachy keen. Thanks." In true Indian style, I should whine, "Ma's arthritis pains her." Nobody's ever peachy keen in India.

"Please inquire after them and extend my fondest regards."

"Thanks, I will." From what century did this man sprout? Even in India, he seemed like a throwback to the nineteenth century.

He steeples his long fingers in front of him. He's waiting, so I keep talking. "And how is your family? Your mother, your relatives?" I ask.

"They're as well as one can expect. Your thoughts are much appreciated." The ensuing silence makes me fidget but doesn't seem to bother him.

He leans forward. "Let's get to why I'm here."

I catch a whiff of his cologne and lean back. I need all my brain cells in working condition. "Why are you here, Mr. Prasad?"

"I must find a wife for Dev."

"Your younger brother?" The one Kali met in India.

He nods. "Our father passed away some time ago. He's therefore unable to approve the match."

"You told me. I'm very sorry."

"Now that Dev has come to America, it's more difficult to

find a good Indian wife. He's tried online matrimonial services. Such sites flourish on the Internet, he says, but thus far, nothing has worked."

"I'm glad you came to me." I bite my bottom lip. I wonder what he means by "a good Indian wife."

He shifts in the chair. "How many marriages have you successfully arranged?"

"I'm not sure how many couples are still together, but Donna and I have introduced hundreds of singles—"

"How long have you been in this line of work?"

"A little over five years," I say. "I helped Lakshmi, the owner, and she grew to trust me."

His lips turn down in a *wow, impressive* expression. "What's your fee?"

Sounds as though he's hiring a hit man. "Varies, depending on whether you want a date for Dev or a marriage partner—"

"Marriage. No time for dates."

"Do you think Dev believes he has time for dates?"

"That is of no consequence," Raja says.

I take a deep breath, give him my fee. I expect him to spit and leave, but he doesn't blink.

"I'll pay twice your price."

My mouth goes dry. I suppose princes have access to gold bars and diamonds and endless wads of cash. "That's a lot of money, Mr. Prasad."

"I said, call me Raja."

"Well, I—"

"The woman must be found immediately. The auspicious date for his wedding approaches in less than six months."

Less than six months? I sit up straight. "I need to check my schedule." *I need to talk to Kali. Now.*

"The woman must be perfect and loyal."

My heart rate picks up. I think of fickle Kali, falling in love every three months, wearing form-fitting dresses with her cleavage spilling out. "No woman is perfect, Mr. Prasad."

"We'll find one who is. Dev must be married."

I tap the eraser end of the pencil on my desk. "Aren't you going about this backward? I mean, isn't the older son supposed to find a wife first?"

"I'm close to my own engagement." His voice is flat, but the words smack me in the face.

The room swirls. "Engaged? Congratulations."

"Nearly. I worry about Dev. A good wife will help him settle."

Questions crowd into my mind. Raja Prasad nearly engaged? I want to ask about his fiancée, but I don't want to seem too interested. I'm not interested. He's handsome, but not my type.

"Women can't change men, Mr. Prasad." I wonder if this young Dev is a player. I think of Kali, starry-eyed, longing for her *desi* Indian wedding.

His eyes twinkle. I'm amusing him. "So do we have a deal?"

"You came all the way from India to ask me to arrange a match for your brother. Couldn't you find a real Bengali matchmaker?"

"You are real."

I glance at the postcards, at the wilting daisies on the bookshelf. I'm not real. My life has become surreal, a soap opera. "Shouldn't we check with your brother? Does he even want to get married?"

"That's irrelevant."

I think of Raja Prasad as a Borg drone on *Star Trek*. He's assimilating me, cell by cell. *Resistance is futile.* "I'm sure it's relevant to *him*. And maybe he's already found someone."

"He's not mentioned anyone."

"Nobody at all?"

Raja shakes his head. "The woman must be young—"

Eighteen to twenty-fourish, I jot down.

"—fair-skinned, traditional. She must speak many languages, preferably Bengali, Hindi, English, and Kannada—"

"Why Kannada?" That rules out Kali.

"Our mother speaks Kannada."

"But isn't this about your brother and his wife? What if he meets the perfect woman for *him*, but she doesn't speak your mother's language?"

"Then the woman is not appropriate."

I can't be attracted to Raja, because his attitude is going to make me throw up. "Okay, Kannada and—"

"She must be educated in the sciences and the arts, interested in world affairs, and she must cook well."

"A real Renaissance woman, huh?" Two strikes against Kali.

"She must excel in domestic affairs." Three strikes.

"Housecleaning? Don't you hire domestic help?"

He blinks, then regains his composure. "She must be willing to run the household."

Superwoman. "If she's educated in the arts and sciences, and she's this amazing scholar, how will she find time for cooking, cleaning, and taking care of a family?"

His lips tighten.

I write furiously, my handwriting messier by the minute.

"She must be capable of bearing children."

"Aren't most women?" I look up at him, we lock gazes, and suddenly there's an embarrassing intimacy between us. I glance at the automatic writing on the page, my cheeks hot.

I feel him watching my hand move across the paper as I write. "And we do not want a woman who was previously married or who already has children. This creates complications."

"Complications. Of course." When I clobber him, he'll have real complications.

"Very well. I shall expect your results in two days." He stands.

"Wait a minute. I haven't agreed to do this. What about what the woman wants? What do I tell her? You didn't fill out a questionnaire. What are Dev's interests, hobbies, his stats—"

"He loves food, wine, reading, movies. Finishing his MBA, as I mentioned. He speaks five languages."

"Impressive. What does he want to do after college?"

"He'll join the family business."

"What if he doesn't want to?"

"That is not an issue."

"Maybe he should come in with you next time. Then I can ask him a few questions."

"Not necessary." A veil of darkness crosses Raja's face. He's about to speak when Donna pops her head in the door. "Lina—" Then she sees Raja Prasad, and her mouth drops open. "Oh, I didn't mean to interrupt."

"You aren't interrupting." I shove my chair back, and it tips over. I'm on the floor. Raja stands quickly but gracefully. In two strides he's beside me, reaching out a hand to help me up. I smooth my hair. "I don't make a habit of falling over like that."

"Perhaps the chair needs repair." Raja gives a pleasant smile.

"Oh, right! The chair. Of course. It's old and decrepit." My ears must be on fire.

Donna sidles in, watching Raja Prasad in awe. "Mrs. Mukerjee is coming today—"

"This is Raja Prasad," I say. "Prince Raja Prasad. We met at my sister's wedding in Kolkata."

Raja glances at me, a flicker of surprise in his eyes. Whoops—I wasn't supposed to know he was a prince. Now he knows I've been inquiring about him. He probably pictures me giggling and gossiping with my girlfriends.

Donna shakes Raja's hand too long. "I'm really, really incredibly happy to meet you. You don't know how happy—"

"The pleasure is mine." He's diplomatic to the molecule.

"Oh, wow." She sways before withdrawing her hand.

Raja turns to me. "Dinner Friday evening. You can give me your decision then."

Donna smiles widely.

"If you need to reach me for any reason, I'm staying at the Hilton," Raja says.

"Fine . . . the Hilton." I shuffle the papers around on my desk, and a couple of file folders slip onto the floor. Dinner?

"Seven o'clock? I have a car in the city. Where should I pick you up?" He strides to the door, waits for my answer.

In desperation, I search my mind for excuses. *I have a big date with the TV. I have to paint my toenails. Clean my windows.* I can't bring myself to tell him I have a fiancé. I would have to lie, and for some unfathomable reason, I can't lie to Raja Prasad. He's a walking truth serum.

"Seven o'clock will be fine," I hear myself say, and then, to my horror, I give him my address.

After he leaves, Donna deflates in the chair and fans herself with a file. "Whoa, I can still smell his cologne, Lina. The man is hot."

"He's not all *that*." My heart is still racing. I feel as though I've just run a marathon.

"Oh, yes, he is."

"He makes a lot of assumptions about people. It's infuriating."

"Did you tell him about Mr. Phantom?" She nods toward the line of gifts and flowers on my shelves.

"It's none of his business. Besides, this isn't a date."

"Think about why you didn't tell him, Lina."

My cheeks heat up again. "I have no interest in Raja Prasad. He's practically engaged."

"Then why did you agree to have dinner with him?"

"I told you. It's business. This is about his brother."

"Yeah, right. If you don't want to go, I'll go. God, I'll go. What should I wear?"

"It's just business. He's traditional. He has no idea what an independent American woman is like."

"You can show him."

"Uh-uh. Not me. I may come up with a few prospects for his brother, and that's it."

I have to talk to Kali.

Eighteen

*K*ali drives me to Golden Gate Park for an emergency jog.

"Dev's brother wants to find him a suitable wife," she shouts. "I could shoot them both in the pills!"

In the language of Austin Powers, she means a swift kick in the balls.

"So . . . you spoke to Dev again?"

"Once, for five minutes. He's still in India, returning to the States next week. It was a bad connection. If only he would meet me again, he'd know. We have chemistry, cross-mojonation." She picks up the pace. Her banana-yellow shorts and tank top leave no curve to the imagination. Her breasts jiggle with each step.

I'm sticking to a T-shirt and fleece jogging pants. "A cross-cultural relationship might not work out, especially because he's a prince. And who knows—he could be a chauvinist. You remember the guy I met at Durga's wedding?"

She nods.

I tell her more about my first meeting with Raja.

"You spoke to Dev's brother? Why didn't you tell me?"

"Raja's sexist. Dev probably is too."

She waves an arm and turns left past the Japanese Tea Garden. "Dev's a good guy. His family runs two orphanages."

I try not to show my shock. Orphanages? I remember the scruffy kitten, and I wonder what else I don't know about Raja Prasad. "Kali, have you told Dev about my engagement?"

She frowns. "It didn't come up. We didn't talk for long. I'm sorry, should I have told him?"

Okay, time to take a risk, go for broke. Kali must know the truth. She's my sister. I share everything with her. I have to come clean. As I talk, weight lifts from my shoulders.

She stops, her chest heaving, hands on her hips. "You made up everything? What about the call from Raja? His stuff all over your apartment?"

I tell her about Harry.

"But Lina, why did you lie?"

"It was a spur-of-the-moment decision, and then I couldn't take it back. Everyone's so happy. Ma, Baba—"

"You're too much. Auntie Kiki's coming soon. What will you do?"

"I've been trying to find a suitable man." I tell her about my disastrous dates. "Please don't tell Dev, or Raja Prasad. Until I figure this out. I do want to find someone, but—"

"They're bound to find out. What if your suitable man isn't named Raja?"

"I'll gracefully inform the family that I've broken off my engagement with Raja, and now I have a new fiancé."

"What about Raja Prasad?" Kali asks. "Do you like him?"

My face heats. "We're from different worlds. He came to my office and asked me to find Dev a wife."

"He *what*?"

"He wants me to arrange the match."

"Did you tell him about Dev and me?"

"You haven't even dated him. Besides, Kali, your relationships pass like tropical storms."

"Whoa. Tell me what you really think." She strides past me toward the parking lot. I run after her.

"I'm sorry. I didn't mean that. If you really like this Dev, then you should meet him again."

She stops at her red Toyota Corolla and jabs the key into the lock. "You'll be introducing him to other women."

"Don't you think his brother ought to know about you? If

Dev really likes you? Raja says he wants a Renaissance woman who speaks five languages, but who'll have babies and stay home and care for the family."

She yanks open the door. I run around to the passenger side and jump in before she drives off without me.

She rests her head on the steering wheel. "I wouldn't mind all that."

I sit back. "All what?"

"Maybe I want kids. Dev says he might move back to India after his MBA. Maybe I want to live in India."

"I didn't know—"

"I never did that well in school. I can barely speak two words in Bengali."

I wrap my arms around her. "Neither can I. Look, maybe you don't speak five languages, but if you and Dev have cross-mojonation, then you ought to meet him again. Go for it."

She straightens up. "Really?"

"What if I arrange the meeting? Between you and Dev Prasad? Then you could meet Raja as well."

"Would you really do that?"

"Yes, I'll do it. If you two are meant to be together, then I'm fulfilling my obligation as a matchmaker."

Nineteen

On Friday, the phone won't leave me alone. I send the calls to voice mail. I'm jumpy. By four o'clock, I'm a basket case. I've all but forgotten I need to find my own real fiancé.

I have nothing to wear. Prince Raja Prasad is taking me to dinner. Does he expect me to wear a sari? What will I tell him? I've decided to take the job, but only if Dev meets Kali, who's foolishly infatuated with your brother?

I can't do it.

I think of Raja Prasad's long eyelashes, his confident manner. His edgy looks. He's a traditional Indian man who wants a traditional Indian wife.

It's only business.

I imagine him showing up in full prince regalia, a couple of humble servants unrolling a red carpet as he escorts me into a plush restaurant where his entire extended family waits, his mother pursing her lips in disgust.

Or maybe he'll take me to some hole-in-the-wall South of Market, just to live as the natives do. I hate this. I can usually control my situation. I can control my fake fiancé, make him appear and disappear. I know what most men want when they step into my office. I assess the way they dress, their mannerisms and mode of speech.

Raja Prasad confounds me. His presence fills the room, making me clumsy and distracted. I drop pens. I trip, spill my tea. On my knees, I use a paper towel to clean up, but the tea is already seeping into the carpet.

Donna comes in, drops a pile of folders on my desk, and kneels to help. "Guess what? You'll be proud of me. I gave you a little help with Mr. Prince."

"What do you mean, 'help'?"

She sits back on her heels. "He called yesterday, after you left. Told me what he wanted, and I spent the whole day doing research."

"What do you mean? What did you do?" I'm suddenly queasy.

"Look at you. You're a mess."

"What did you do?"

"I accepted his offer, of course. For both of us. We're a team, aren't we? It's good money. Twice the fee. I e-mailed him some prospects today."

"You gave him profiles? Of women?"

"I'm so proud of myself. I worked like a maniac. Raja Prasad will do that to a girl, won't he?" She winks.

Hair falls in my eyes. "You have no idea what you've done!"

"He's only here for a short time. We have to find a wife for his brother right away."

"Donna, you should've spoken to me first."

She gives me a knowing look. "I'm handing it over to you now. You have a good time tonight, okay? And keep your cool. Mr. Prince has you flustered."

"I'm not flustered. I'm never flustered. I'm always perfectly composed." Splotches of tea stain my white shirt. "It's my sister, Kali. She met Dev in India. She's infatuated with him. I promised to set them up on a date, but now—ah, well. It's not your fault."

Donna's mouth forms an O. "I screwed up. I'm sorry . . ."

I push the hair back from my face. "It's okay. You didn't know. I can still set up the meeting." When I tell him about Kali, he'll flip. But I have to do this for her.

Donna gets up. "Get going. I'll take care of things here."

I try to remember her words as a mantra. *Have a good time tonight.* What is a good time, exactly, with a man like Raja Prasad?

At home, I purge my closet of its usual suspects. The maroon dress has to go. It makes me resemble a bruised apple. The eighties lime green dress with the linebacker shoulder pads? The miniskirt with white go-go boots? A frilly peasant blouse from my seventies kick? My wardrobe needs a serious makeover. Once again, clothes are strewn on the bed in a pile for the Salvation Army. What if I show up in ripped jeans and a "Bite Me" T-shirt, just to piss off Mr. Chauvinist?

I stare at the red lace teddy. Maybe I should wear nothing but that and high heels. We'll end up naked in his hotel room. He'll dim the lights, bring two glasses of champagne to the bedside table, then—

What am I thinking?

I'd better choose a fancy outfit. We must be going to an expensive restaurant. Do I own anything elegant? Perhaps the black cocktail dress that fits with a certain tightness in the hips and rear. Too boring and predictable? If I wear a nice jacket over it and don't sit down too fast, I should survive the evening without any rips. Screw the stockings.

Good for you. Taking a stand.

"Oh, no, not you again." I groan, not wanting to imagine my phantom fiancé standing behind me, but his breath caresses my neck.

Are you two-timing me? This seems serious.

"Business dinner."

Then why don't you wear a suit?

I'm already struggling to squeeze into the dress. I perform amazing feats of yoga to stretch the fabric over my waist, and then I stop.

"You're right. A suit. It's business. Just business!" I yell at myself in the mirror. What if I wear the red lace teddy under the suit? I'll feel sexy, and Raja will never know.

Are you sure you don't want him to know?

I squirm out of the dress, put on the teddy beneath a black suit jacket and pants. Snazzy, with a low-cut blouse. My most daring combo, but I still don't have much cleavage. So what? Do I want Mr. Chauvinist to look at my boobs? I slap my forehead. I don't care what he looks at. I want his hulking shape, those broad shoulders, perfectly formed biceps, those penetrating eyes, to find me completely unappealing.

But he pursued me across continents. What does that mean, exactly? He's here for his brother, not me. And I'm here for Kali.

I yank a brush through my frizzy hair. Did he really choose me, or was I merely convenient? I shouldn't read too much into his decision to look me up. I gave him the name of my company, after all—

The phone rings, and adrenaline rushes through me. I press my hand to my chest. I'm having a heart attack. I pick up the receiver, hold it in midair. What if it's him, canceling the dinner? I can't decide whether to be relieved or disappointed when my mother's demanding voice cuts through the line.

"Lina? Where are you? Are you there?"

I picture her standing in the marble foyer, the domed ceiling overhead, sunrays from the skylight falling on her black hair. She's probably wearing jeans, and she has a cup of tea in her other hand. I don't know why she doesn't sit in the kitchen. She always uses the cordless telephone in the hall.

I put the phone to my ear. "Yes, Ma. I can't talk long. I'm going out."

"Going out? So Raja has returned from traveling?"

I wince at the sound of Raja's name. "No, he's still away. This is a business dinner."

"What kind of business?"

"What kinds are there, Ma?"

"Why is Raja not back yet? Are you sure you've made the right decision?"

"You'll meet him." I try to push aside the image of Auntie Kiki pursing her lips. "Please, Ma, I'm in no mood to be interrogated tonight. What do you want?"

"You are so rude to your mother. She calls you to chat, and all you can say is, 'What does she want?'"

I hate it when she refers to herself in the third person.

"I'm sorry, Ma." I sit on the bed.

"I'm calling about Baba." She lowers her voice, which still echoes. My parents live in a sprawling mansion, and still she can't find privacy. "He's ill again."

"Ill with what?"

"You know how his stomach is. We went out for dinner last night, and he came home with the pains."

"Indigestion, Ma. He always has indigestion."

"Stomach pains could mean a lot of things, Pupu."

Oh, no—not that name again. I wish I could stuff the word into a capsule and launch it into space. "If you think it's something worse, he should see a doctor."

"Shhh," she says, as if he can hear me from the second floor. "He *is* a doctor. He makes the worst patient. He took antacid, and now he's resting. Perhaps, I'm thinking, he was having another type of pain."

"What are you talking about? You mean like another ulcer?"

"Psychological pains. He's all the time worrying about you and Kali. Mainly about you."

"*I'm* giving Baba indigestion? I'm not even there, Ma." I roll my eyes toward the ceiling. I want to yank out my hair. How does she always manage to twist the situation to make it my fault?

"He worries about your wedding. He must meet Raja. You talk to Baba, nah? He'll feel much better if he hears your voice." I hear the tap-tap echo of footsteps. She's walking upstairs with the phone. "You tell Baba he'll meet Raja when Auntie Kiki is here. He'll be so happy you're both coming."

I grit my teeth during the pause, then a raspy voice comes on the line. "Lina, baby? Where are you?"

"I'm home, Baba. In my apartment. How're you feeling?"

"Oh, I'm all right." His voice is slow and tired.

"You don't sound all right. You rest, okay? Have you got a doctor's appointment?"

"When are you coming?" He ignores my question.

"Soon, Baba. For your birthday."

"You'll bring Raja, nah?"

"I'll see."

"All the time you're giving your Baba a hard time." His voice is fading. "What am I to do with you?"

"Baba, just rest. You'll get worse if you don't take care."

"How do you like your job?"

I shift the phone to the other ear. "It's peachy."

"You're not considering studying for your Ph.D.?"

"I don't need a doctorate to be a matchmaker." My throat tightens.

"You've done your B.A. Why not keep going?"

"I probably wouldn't study psychology. Baba, I can't talk about this now—"

"You pick one profession, you stick with it. Follow through to the end. That's what my generation did, Pupu."

"My generation has more options." I feel as though I'm ten years old again, stumbling in classical Indian dance class, the heavy silver *ghungroos* clanking like prison chains around my ankles. I could never dance well enough to please Baba.

"No point in choosing another career if you can't do it properly, nah?" he says.

I'm little Pupu again, stomping my feet. *I'm a good matchmaker.* "You're wise, Baba," I say instead. His disapproval bleeds through the phone, drips in a puddle on my floor.

"I always said, if you couldn't study medicine, psychology is a perfectly acceptable alternative. You could do applied research."

"Look, Baba, I'd love to keep talking, but I'm going out—"

"With this Raja? Is he a good man? Will he set you straight?"

"He'll keep me on track."

"Ah—what a relief. We must meet Raja before Kiki arrives. If she thinks you're without a husband, now, *that* would kill her dead."

I count to three and blink back tears. Then I speak in a measured tone. "Baba, I have to go. I'll call you tomorrow, okay? Give Ma my love." I hang up before he has a chance to berate me. My hands are shaking.

I pace and practice my breathing exercises. I haven't been to yoga class in weeks, and tension tugs at my chest. Auntie Kiki raised Baba after his mother passed away. In his eyes, Auntie's a goddess whose breath bestows life.

I dab my face with a damp cloth, put on eyeliner and lipstick. That will have to do. I'm already late. I grab my purse and rush out into the cool night air.

Twenty

A silver Lexus waits at the curb. Raja Prasad emerges from the driver's side and opens the passenger door for me. How can he look so good in everything he wears? Black suit, black shirt, black tie, casual yet elegant and sexy, like a wardrobe from the Alan Truong collection. I instantly imagine him as the bridegroom—what am I thinking?

He says nothing. No *you're beautiful, you look nice.* But I feel as though he's already whispered all kinds of forbidden things in my ear when I slip in beside him, the smell of Lexus mixed with his mysterious spicy cologne.

"Thank you for coming." He starts the engine and steers into traffic.

I pull the seatbelt across my lap. "Where are we going?"

"Have you heard of Herbert Winton?"

My mouth drops open. "The chef? We're going to Joie de Vivre?"

"You know of it." His voice slides over and settles across my shoulders.

"I've never been there."

"Neither have I, but I hear it's the best restaurant in the city."

"I'm underdressed."

"You're fine."

Fine, not beautiful. Sweat breaks out on my forehead. "If you say so."

"I trust you had a productive day?" His right eyebrow rises.

"Quite. Thank you." I think of the spilled tea.

I should tell him I have a fiancé who shares his first name. No, I shouldn't. After he parks the car, I do my most businesslike walk into Joie de Vivre and consider my options. Come clean or say nothing.

I work myself up into a tizzy, barely noticing the lavishly decorated restaurant as we enter the main dining area. The room is draped in Chantal fabric in shades of gold and green.

The host seats us at a table near the back. I glance at the

other guests, all clad in designer dresses and suits and laden with understated, overpriced jewelry. Only a few silvery threads float between lovers. The scents of expensive floral colognes and sharp aftershave lotions mingle in the air. It's enough to send my nose into a coma.

Raja resembles a dashing adventurer, even in the suit. "Would you like wine?"

I nod, open the menu, glance at the walls, at the luxurious oil paintings, up at the crystal chandelier. Everything glitters. I need sunglasses.

When the waiter arrives, Raja orders a bottle of chardonnay from the Clos MiMi winery, then fixes his gaze on me.

I open the menu and start babbling. "The French eat a lot of meat, don't they? Duck, quail, veal. Did you know veal calves are kept in small crates? They can't turn around. They're fed nothing but gruel. They're denied water, so they keep trying to drink the gruel and get fatter and fatter, and then . . . oh." I clap a hand over my mouth. "I'm so sorry. I'm sure you didn't want to hear all that."

"You are disarmingly honest. I neglected to ask whether you're vegetarian."

"Uh, it's okay. There are plenty of vegetarian options on the menu. Are you vegetarian?"

"No, but I don't eat veal either."

"Oh, good, then. So. Uh."

"How about the heirloom tomato feast?"

"'A colorful sampler.'" I can't help grinning, and then I notice he's grinning too, which makes his face suddenly more open and friendly and twice as handsome.

"As you may notice"—he lowers his voice and leans toward me—"there's an entirely separate vegetarian tasting menu." He pulls the smaller menu from the bigger one and hands it to me. "Open it. You'll see the heirloom tomato *symphony*."

"How do you suppose that differs from the tomato *feast?*"

"The symphony has tomato violins?" He grins, and I smile. A silver-haired couple at the next table frowns at us. The man looks a bit like my father. I imagine Baba lying in bed with psychological pains, then push the picture from my mind. I won't feel guilty tonight.

"Trio of petite peas soup," I read. "Better not order that one."

"You might get only a trio of peas." He chuckles.

"Japanese eggplant stuffed with Sardinian couscous."

"What makes Sardinian couscous different from Milan couscous, or La Maddalena couscous or Sicilian couscous?" Raja asks in a serious tone, and then laughs.

"Oh, this is the entire vegetarian five-course meal. You have to order everything. I'll be a beluga whale by the time we roll out of here."

"I'll be a killer whale." He chuckles again. Suddenly I imagine Raja and me at Milton's Diner near my apartment.

We'll munch on homemade French fries and drink organic strawberry milkshakes.

We're still chuckling when the waiter comes. We straighten our faces, and Raja orders. The silver-haired woman at the next table casts me another tight look, then lifts a fork to her mouth, closes her lips daintily around a square of cheese, and chews. Her husband gulps his wine and stares off somewhere to the left of her ear, his eyes glazed.

I realize, then, that she reminds me of myself when I sat across from Dr. Dilip Dutta. Bored, trying to make the evening work. I wasn't wearing a red lacy teddy that night. Now I'm wearing one under the power suit. I'm like a Russian matryoshka doll. If you remove the outer nested dolls, you'll eventually reach the sexy inner doll.

I wonder if Raja senses the inner doll, satin caressing its skin. I wonder if this is the time to tell him about Kali. No, I'll wait. I'm Cinderella at the ball, and I don't want to disturb the mood.

Our appetizer comes, a plate of colorful aromatic tomatoes. As we eat, Raja manages to extract my most intimate childhood stories. I talk about school, about excelling in English and classical piano, especially Bach's Inventions. I tell him about my privacy phase at age seven, when I had to make sure everyone knew I was in the bathroom, so they wouldn't come in, and I always locked the door.

"Then once, after we'd gone hiking, I sat on the toilet and

found a tick on my thigh. I ran outside with my pants down, yelling for my father."

"You were a bold contradiction even then."

I'll take that as flattery. A smile touches my lips. "Baba was talking to the neighbors. He pulled the tick off my leg. What about you? Where did you grow up? Did you have ticks?"

"I've always lived in Kolkata, although my family is originally from Assam. No ticks in the city, but we have mosquitoes, the occasional snake, dogs, cats, house geckos—"

"There was a gecko in my room, the night of Durga's wedding." I run a finger around the rim of my wineglass. "Creepy—"

"They're harmless." He signals the waiter for more water. I wonder if Raja is harmless, too, whether he only looks dangerous. "I grew up with geckos. My parents kept their main flat in Kolkata. We spent holidays in our cottage in Santiniketan and in Puri, by the sea."

"You have many homes."

"Only three."

"Sounds like a dream. We spent summers camping up through the redwood forest, or flying to Oahu so our parents could play tennis."

"You and your sisters didn't play?" He says the word *play* as though it means many things. He leans forward, and I catch another whiff of his spicy aftershave.

"Durga did. She was always athletic. All she could think about was running, jumping, and hitting things with racquets. Kali hoarded piles of *Seventeen* and *Cosmopolitan* magazines and carried a makeup bag as big as a suitcase."

"And you?"

"I swam. You can be alone in the water, if you swim out far enough—"

"Why do you swim out far, Lina? Trying to catch a riptide?" He lowers his voice, and for a moment, I feel as though he knows me too well. When did I start swimming out far? After Nathu died?

"The sea's comforting," I say.

"Sometimes I want to do the same, float with the currents."

"Then you're like me. Most people stay near the shoreline."

"In some respects, you stay near the shore too, Lina Ray." He pours me another glass of wine. "You play it safe. You're not engaged, I assume?"

He's asking me directly, and I can't answer. My vocal cords shrivel. I croak, but no words come out. *I made up a fiancé who's a little like you.* "No husband," I say. That's not a lie, is it?

"Why? Afraid you'll find the right man?"

I'm playing with my earring again. "I'm a career woman. I work, see friends, practice yoga, go to movies, hike, and I read a lot. I don't have time for a husband." Wait—I'm supposed to ask the questions. "What about you? What are your hobbies?" Oh, please. What a boring question.

"I'm a big reader too. Mainly Bengali authors, but also some Western writers. I have eclectic tastes."

"Eclectic, as in, you read *USA Today* as well as *Penthouse*, or—"

"I absorb all genres." He opens his hands, palms forward.

"What about your brother Dev? A big reader?" There I go, asking boring questions again.

"He prefers teaching cricket to American girls."

"So he's a lady's man." A strike against Dev.

"How can he help it if the girls flock to him?"

"Do I detect a note of jealousy?"

"Between brothers? Never." He grins. On him, a grin is multifaceted, like colors through a prism. My insides buzz with warmth.

"So it was just you and your brother growing up?" I ask.

"Our parents and various aunts, uncles, cousins—"

"Of course. You're never alone in India, right?"

"I'm accustomed to having family around all the time. America is a vast land of opportunity, to be sure, but it's also a great land of loneliness."

"Do you think I'm lonely?" I scoop couscous onto my plate.

"There's a forlorn air about you. A shadow."

The air thickens in my throat. If he could only see my shadow, my imaginary man. "I have family here. I'm not lonely. But we all live in different parts of the country."

"Connected only by plane, nah? In India, we're usually close to each other, although I also have relatives in Mumbai and Chennai. I should never like to grow old in America."

I nearly choke on a mouthful of couscous. So Raja Prasad will never move to America. Not that I want him to. "Why not?"

"Is it true you throw your parents into rest homes?" His left eyebrow rises all by itself. How does it do that? How does he stare as if his eyes harbor tiny X-ray machines to photograph my soul?

"We don't exactly *throw* them. And they're called retirement communities, not rest homes. It's hard to find time for family here. People are so busy with their careers, their frenetic daily lives—" I stare at the rippling reflection in my wineglass. I'm one of those frenetic people. Would I throw Ma and Baba into a retirement home? I would never do such a thing, and they wouldn't let their children make decisions for them. "Many people *want* to move into retirement communities. They make new friends their own age, play shuffleboard, go to movies together—"

"It seems unnatural. We never dream of abandoning family to such places. My parents—they were a love marriage. They fell for each other at the Samode Palace in Rajasthan, one of the most intimate places in India. They grew more deeply in love over time, and they planned to grow old together. Now that my father has died, my mother would never dream of leaving the home she shared with him in Kolkata. I live there too, when I'm not traveling."

A dollop of couscous falls off my fork and plops on the plate. Raja lives with his mother? "In America, grown men who live with their mothers are often considered peculiar."

He stops, his wineglass suspended halfway to his mouth. "Do you consider me peculiar?"

"Not at all." Sexy, strange, fascinating, not what I expected. But not peculiar. "But I can't imagine living with my Baba and Ma." Baba would offer daily career advice. He could run his own "Ask Baba" column in the newspaper. "Anyway, they've made their own plans. They're saving for retirement. They're not relying on their daughters to take care of them."

"I suppose this is wise, nah?" Raja downs his wine. "You must take care of yourself in this country."

"We don't have servants or drivers, if that's what you mean. Some affluent families hire nannies for their children."

"I had an ayah, the equivalent of a nanny. She still lives with us, cooks and cleans. She and my mother are like sisters."

Like sisters, huh? My insides frown while my mouth sticks in a polite smile. "Your ayah is still a servant."

"You have a point. But such arrangements make all our lives easier."

"We didn't have servants. I started making my own bed when I was two."

"So you've always been an independent female."

Why does independence feel like loneliness right now? When I leave for work each morning, my apartment freezes in time. When I return home in the evening, nothing has changed. My teacup still sits on the countertop next to a bowl of soggy Lucky Charms.

Sometimes I wish a house elf lived under my bed. She could pop out while I'm away and rearrange the furniture, cook, clean, and open my mail, so the apartment will look lived-in when I come home. I wasn't lonely when I had boyfriends or roommates, but their habits often annoyed me. I hid in my room for the comfort of solitude. Now I imagine Raja sharing my space, reading my newspaper, using my towels, drinking my tea.

I shove the images under my napkin. "In India, I might come home to a swept room, folded laundry, servants flitting about the house, relatives yelling," I say in a rush. "I'm drawn to my homeland, and yet I can't live among all those people."

His face closes, his emotions retreating into darkness. "Americans tend to find India—overwhelming."

"I'd like to find a happy medium."

"You've been back to India often?" Raja asks.

"Just a few times. Do you come to America often?"

"On business. For the first eighteen years of my life, I never traveled beyond India."

He acts as though I'm interviewing him for a job. For what position? Business partner, friend, lover?

"Where did you go to school?" I ask. At an upscale institute for royalty, I presume.

"When I was quite young, my parents sent me off to boarding school in Darjeeling, in the Himalayas. Huge stone building, like a castle, gothic." He gestures in a sweeping motion with his arms. "A bit like the school in *Harry Potter*. Boys came from all over the world, from the families of Tibetan gold smugglers, from America's blue blood. I found my place among them. My brother stayed back in Kolkata. Our mother couldn't bear to be without both her sons. I learned to accept living away from home, for a time."

I picture him as a strapping young man in a woolen school uniform. He probably trekked through blizzards, rappelled from ice cliffs. He must've been an accomplished mountain climber, braving the storms of Mount Everest. His girlfriends were probably princesses and daughters of rich international jet-setters.

"So now, how long will you be here?" I ask.

"Just a few weeks. This is my last stop before returning home. I've been trying to bring my mother over for a visit. She wants to see where Dev goes to university. She's been to the East Coast. This time, we've hit a snag with her visa. New security regulations. I'm working on it."

I regard Raja in a new way. The loyal son. If I were a mother, I'd love to have a son like him. I wonder, have I done all I can to support my parents? I touch the gold brooch pinned to my shirt. I've been wearing it on all my dates. I can't let Ma down.

"Will you have time to show your mother around?" I ask. "I mean, with your work and all?"

"Actually, I'm fund-raising for my charitable projects. I run two orphanages outside Kolkata."

"You what?" I plunk down my glass, splashing merlot on the white linen tablecloth. The blushing stain spreads.

Raja reaches over to dab at the spill with his napkin. "We give girls a chance at an education, a life of independence. Unfortunately, many Indian families still value boys more than girls."

My mind stretches to absorb this new information. Kali mentioned that his family financed orphanages, but I never dreamed that Raja was so personally involved in the charitable work. Raja Prasad, Mr. Playboy of the Far Pavilions, helping orphaned girls achieve independence? My fingers itch to touch his sleeve, make sure he's real.

I glance down at my plate. The time has passed so quickly. We've already had dessert, and I barely noticed. I'm Cinderella dancing with the prince.

On the drive home, my magical carriage becomes a pumpkin again when Raja turns to me, his voice all business. "I've brought the files from Donna. Where shall we go to study them?"

Twenty-one

$\mathcal{I}$ curl my fingers over the door handle. "Would you like to come up to my place?"

He nods. I can't read his expression in the darkness.

At my apartment, my fingers tremble as I unlock the door. What will he think of my modest abode? Its greatest assets are large bay windows and hardwood floors. I've returned most of Harry's things. No telltale signs linger. At least, I hope not, and I'm glad my bedroom door is closed, so Raja can't see my bras hanging over the bedpost, my underwear atop piles of dirty clothes.

"You have a lovely flat." He steps inside.

"Would you like coffee, tea?"

"Tea."

A man after my own heart.

I set the kettle to boil, and we sit on the couch.

"Raja, I—" My body tenses. Better to be out with it now. "I'd like Dev to meet my sister, Kali."

He raises an eyebrow. "Ah, Kali. Dev mentioned her. I have not discounted her."

I let out a long breath of relief. He knows. Okay, that's a start. I sit back. Play it cool. Don't say, What about what Kali and Dev want? Don't push. Not yet. "So you're willing to meet her?"

"Perhaps. We'll look at these files."

"She's smart, sincere, and beautiful. She has a great job." I nearly say, She and Dev have cross-mojonation.

Raja opens the first file and pulls out a photograph of a fair-skinned, sultry young thing with longish hair. He reads, "Shree, eighteen, wants a career in computers. Subcaste Kayastha, non-vegetarian. She wants to be financially independent and establish herself professionally." He pauses. "She's not appropriate."

"Because she's not Brahmin? You still worry about caste?"

"In the modern world, such affiliations matter less, nah?" He frowns, as if he disapproves of this trend.

"I rarely think about caste, Raja. My only indication of caste is my surname, Ray. Otherwise"—I wave my arm to encompass all of America—"caste doesn't matter here."

"Every culture labels strata and ethnic groups, and yet scholars focus undue attention on India."

"Are you saying you approve of caste structure?" My fingernails dig into the couch.

"Not in the least." His eyes twinkle with amusement. "I'm merely playing devil's advocate. My family also became Brahmo Samaj. We reject the caste system."

My fingers relax. "Why didn't you say so? Brahmo Samaj. That's great. I didn't know. But . . . can princes be Brahmo Samaj?"

"We can be anything we want." He gives me a penetrating look.

"Then why isn't this pretty girl, Shree, appropriate?" My fingers play with a loose thread of fabric on the couch.

"She's simply too young."

The kettle whistles in the kitchen. I leap to my feet and rush off to pour the tea. I arrange the teapot, cups, milk, and sugar on my only tray. I tuck my hair behind my ears and take several deep breaths. Raja Prasad throws off my center of gravity. I'll have to do yoga nonstop for a month to recover.

I return to the living room and sit a little farther from him on the couch. He brings out the next file, with a photograph of a demure woman in a deep red *churidar kurta* and white shawl, her hair tied back, *bindi* on her forehead. "It's a faraway shot. What does she have to hide?" he asks.

"A scar?"

"She's coming here for studies. She already has her master's in Bengali from the University of West Bengal. She's too old."

"Kali's already twenty-five," I say.

"*Acha.*" He takes one spoon of sugar and loads of milk, and brings out file after file. "This one is beautiful. Uma. Her parents say she's soft-spoken, sings, and recites well. Likes to watch movies and listen to Rabindrasangeet. Confident, fun-loving." His right eyebrow rises. "Confidence is good. Shall we set up a meeting?"

Tension scrapes the air between us. "Look, Raja. Donna accepted your offer. She's my colleague. She's a pro. She worked at another agency in Seattle before coming to us three years ago. You should work with her."

"I prefer to work with you."

"I rarely decline such challenging assignments, but this time, I can't do it."

"Why not? I need your keen eye. Your judgment. You've successfully matched many other couples."

"I'm Kali's sister. It's a conflict of interest."

"Please, you must do this."

I stare at Raja for a long moment. He said "please." "My sister likes Dev, and yet you'd have me arrange a meeting between Uma and Dev?"

"Not immediately. You and I can meet Uma and her parents. We'll also arrange a meeting between Dev and Kali. If they're meant to be, they're meant to be. If not, we'll consider Uma. Not very mathematical."

"No," I say, "but then love can't be quantified, can it?"

"What do you think?"

"Okay," I say against my better judgment, against every sane, rational argument I can muster. "I'll do it."

"Good, good." Raja kisses the back of my hand, and my skin tingles at the touch of his lips. "Call me when you've arranged the meeting with Uma's parents."

Then he leaves.

I peel off the suit and the red teddy. How could the night have thrown me for such a curve? Raja seemed opaque, old world, when I first met him. Now I've scraped away the surface to reveal complex depths. Okay, so he doesn't believe in the caste system. He still employs a servant to cook and clean. He still has an ayah. He's still traditional, still a prince, and he's nearly engaged to someone else.

Twenty-two

Well, that was a slam-bang success. My imaginary man shows up in my office wearing a white suit to match the sunshine and breeze outside. *You sure you want to go through with this?*

I set my jaw as I peruse Uma's personality profile. "It's perfectly safe. Raja Prasad and I are meeting Uma's parents at their home this afternoon—"

You're going with Raja Prasad? Let him go alone. You have to find your own fiancé. You shouldn't be working on Saturday, anyway.

"That's none of your business." Mr. Sen wants to see me. Says it's urgent.

144

I'm merely concerned. Where was I last night? I disappeared. He paces in front of my desk. His image has morphed. He's a few inches taller, his shoulders a little wider, and he walks with a slight swagger. His skin darkens to an edgy tan. He's no longer Nathu. His physique is beginning to resemble Raja Prasad's. "You look . . . different," I say. "And your hair. You're combing it on the left now."

He shrugs. *Wasn't my idea. You altered me in your journal last night.*

"I did no such thing. I wrote about Raja Prasad."

Exactly. Why are you giving him so much space? Dr. Dutta left a message, and you never called him back.

"He doesn't have time to date. What he needs is sleep. Go away."

My imaginary man begins to fade.

Mr. Sen waltzes in, radiating confidence in his too-tight gray slacks and a casual sweater with a picture of the Golden Gate Bridge sewn into the front.

"I'm most pleased with my latest date, Miss Chatterjee." He sits and taps the arms of the chair.

"That's nice." I mentally search my files. Oh, yes. Donna left a note. Miss Chatterjee called to say she wasn't interested. How easy it is to dump someone if you don't have to face him or her. You can leave the dirty work to me.

"Will you set me up on another date? Or may I ring her myself?"

"Mr. Sen. I. Uh." I tap my pencil on the desk in time to his tapping. Together we make a symphony. "I don't know how to say this." I search for words that won't disappoint him. *Ms. Chatterjee died. Went bungee jumping. Moved to Taiwan.* It's the first time I've seen his eyes shine, and he didn't use as much oil in his hair today.

"What is it?" He taps faster.

I stare out at the dazzling day. "Miss Chatterjee wants time to think. She says you're not right for her."

The happy sunlight leaks from his face. "She wants a husband with hundred thousand or two hundred thousand salary."

"She doesn't care about money." She says the spark isn't there. "According to Vedic astrology, your charts don't match. There's no connection between the two of you."

"Astrology? Connection? What's this you're saying?"

I don't see the silver thread, but I see the disappointment in his eyes. "The two of you aren't a match."

Mr. Sen raises his arms in frustration. "Who cares about the damned alignment of stars and all that ridiculous, hocus-pocus hogwash? I want to see Ms. Chatterjee, and no quack astrologer will keep her from me."

I sit back, stunned at the determination flaring in his eyes. I clear my throat. "Well, if you insist—"

"She does not give me a chance."

"I can't give you a date unless she agrees to it."

"Then I'll call her myself." He shoves his chair back and leaps to his feet.

"Mr. Sen—"

"I'll get back to you." He strides out, shoulders squared against the world. Where did this new man come from? His personality profile gives his height, weight, skin color, preferences, and income. His measurements and stats are disembodied numbers on paper, but together, they make up an entirely different whole. There's a new energy in Mr. Sen that can't fit into a pen and be written in ink or snapped as a digital photograph. Mr. Sen is a warrior.

I open the file and look at the glossy photograph of Dev Prasad sitting beside Raja on the balcony of a Kolkata flat. Dev is a slimmer, darker, long-haired version of Raja. Raja is wearing khaki, and he has one foot up on the iron railing, a cigar between thumb and forefinger. What type of man is he, really?

Twenty-three

$\mathcal{M}$y brother is still in India, so we've come in his stead."
Raja Prasad and I sit across from Uma Dewan's parents in
their split-level home in the Sunset District, along the city's
western edge.

"Thank you for coming. We are very concerned about our
daughter finding a good husband." Mr. Dewan took the day
off work for this momentous occasion.

"She must've hit traffic," Mrs. Dewan says, pouring four
cups of tea on a brass platter on the coffee table.

I imagine Uma Dewan hurtling through the air, bouncing
from car to car, hitting traffic. I peer through a narrow open-

ing in the heavy curtains. Faint light seeps into the room. Out here in the avenues, trees are sparse, concrete stretches to the horizon, and the wind whips in from the Pacific Ocean. This edge of San Francisco has a washed-out, forgotten feeling.

Mrs. Dewan purses her lips and hands me a cup of steaming tea. She's traditional in a sari, hair tied back, face an unremarkable lump of dough. She sits primly, right next to Mr. Dewan, who wears a hand-knit sweater and slacks. Both are gray-haired, with dark rings under their eyes.

I try to imagine what their life was like in India. "You're both from Chennai?" I ask.

"Beautiful place." Mr. Dewan stares at a spot above my head. "On the Coromandel Coast. White sand beaches, sunshine so bright and hot. A different quality to the light. You've been there?"

"No, but I've seen pictures of palm trees and the ancient temples." I glance down at my hands, clasped in my lap. The faint odors of mold and mothballs pervade the air. I imagine dusty memories of Chennai tucked into shoe boxes in the Dewans' closets.

Raja clears his throat. "How long have you both lived in the States?"

Mrs. Dewan glances at a crack in the ceiling, and her lips move, counting. The whites of her eyes are threaded with tiny red veins. "We came here twenty-five years back," she says. The South Indian accent lingers in her throat. "Such a long time ago." She places knobby fingers over her husband's hairy hand. He nods in agreement.

"Have you been back?" I ask. I focus on a painting mounted on the wall behind the couch—the blue Lord Krishna as a child, pudgy and playful.

"We go back every few years," Mr. Dewan says. "Always Chennai will be home, but we've been here in the States such a long time. It would be difficult to move back to India. There is such a difference to life here, more freedom to find good jobs, and yet—"

"My whole family lives in Chennai," Mrs. Dewan says, and pulls her hand back into her lap.

"You must miss them," I say.

"Very much," she whispers.

And I, who was born there, can return only as a tourist to the country of my ancestry. In India, the languages, the temples, the colorful saris in a myriad of styles, the religions, the complex, ancient culture—it's all as alien to me as it is to any American. And yet, there are things Indian about me, seeds my parents planted. The way we drank thick, sweet *cha* in bed in the morning on weekends, the curry and *samosas* we served on special occasions, the trips back to India, the Bengali my parents spoke to each other at home, their underlying assumptions—that all three girls would marry in our twenties—the India-ghosts haunting us, working their way into our subconscious minds.

My life has been a mix of India and America, and yet I cannot extract one from the other. My mother cooked Campbell's tomato soup as easily as she fried *baigan* and *vindaloo*. Which belongs to her? Where is home to her? To me? I'm not half-and-half. I'm something new altogether.

Here in the dreary avenues, I sense the Dewans' life force bleeding out onto the sidewalks, sliding into the storm drains. This home is a fortress to hold the West at bay.

The longer I sit here, the more trapped I feel, the more I collapse upon myself. I sense reticence in Raja Prasad as well, but he still projects an air of arrogance in the sagging armchair next to me.

Cups clink as we sip our tea in awkward silence, and then a car rumbles into the garage below us. The house shakes as if an earthquake has struck. Soon the woman in question bursts in, wearing jeans and a pullover, her long hair in tendrils around her face. She looks ten years younger than she did in her photograph.

She squints at Raja and me. "Got stuck in traffic. Who are you?"

"We've been waiting twenty minutes, Uma," her father says.

She shrugs. "Can I control traffic? Can I? There was a fucking tanker overturned on the Bay Bridge. I hate coming home to the fifth degree."

Her mother flinches. "Uma, darling. We did mention the matchmaker would be coming this afternoon."

"Oh, right. Better get it over with. I'll be right back." Uma sighs, and I catch a whiff of stale smoke on her clothes. I thought she was a nonsmoker. She stomps off in a huff.

"She is the same Uma in the photograph?" Raja asks.

"No other." Her father nods his head sideways.

"This is why we're worried," Mrs. Dewan says. "We're thinking a good marriage will take care of this problem."

I try not to look at Raja. My fingers curl around the teacup. A series of noises—doors slamming, music blaring, heavy objects dropping with thuds—emanates from upstairs, and then Uma emerges, physically transformed. How could she put on a sari and *bindi* so quickly?

She slumps on the couch next to her parents and stares down Raja and me as if we're rival outlaws at the OK Corral.

"I can't tell you how sick I am of living here. I can't wait to get out of the house, so I might consider your offer." She grabs the teapot, pours herself tea as if it's whisky, and downs the whole cup in one noisy gulp.

"You're prepared to move back to India?" Raja asks, although we've not actually made an offer.

She stops the cup in midair. "What?" She looks at her parents in horror. "I gotta go to India to marry this guy?"

"To live." Raja steeples his fingers, his elbows resting on the arms of his chair.

"To live?" she parrots, her voice shrill.

Her shock reverberates in my bones.

"Your profile shows you're adept at all household tasks. You're prepared to clean, cook, and care for your mother-in-law?"

I glance at Raja Prasad. Is he really asking those questions? Can't he tell she's not the one? I could be her, sitting awkwardly in that sari.

She slams her teacup down on the saucer and glares at her parents. "I'm not moving to India. You said I would move?"

Her mother winces.

Her father's expression doesn't change. "Uma, you're adept, if you put your mind to it."

"I'm not cleaning some guy's house because he's too lazy to clean up after himself. I live here. I grew up here. Why would I want to fly back and live in some backward place where people don't even use toilet paper?"

I stare at Uma. She could be my alter ego.

Mrs. Dewan gives us an apologetic look. "You see why I believe she'll do well in India? She needs discipline."

The blood drains from my face. How could Donna have misjudged this girl? She doesn't belong with Dev.

Raja stands. "Thank you for your time."

We scramble to our feet.

"That's all?" Mr. Dewan says. "When will she meet your brother?"

"I hope never." Uma bites her lip and shifts from foot to

foot. Either she's impatient to leave, or she has to go to the bathroom.

"We'll be in touch." Raja takes Uma's hand and kisses the back of it in his usual smooth gesture. The parents follow us to the door and wave as we walk down the street, then they disappear into their darkened home.

An unexplainable melancholy wafts through me as I look back at the house, now bland and unreadable behind its closed curtains. Have Uma's parents lost her? Why does she still live at home? I can imagine the verbal abuse she rains on them, and how they take it because she's the only family they have here.

Raja stops next to the Lexus, but doesn't get in.

"Look," I say. "I'm sorry about Uma. She wasn't anything like her profile. Sometimes American-born Indians reject their heritage. It's hard not to. The pressures are all around you. Kids leave home early. They're legally independent at eighteen. I bet her friends all have jobs and apartments—"

"This does not excuse the way she spoke to her elders. Her poor mother, pining for her family. Can her daughter not see her pain? Ah well, sometimes people are not who we think they are." He offers his arm. "Shall we walk? The day is young."

Here we are, in the middle of the avenues. We've just met a strange young woman who isn't who I thought she was. Mr. Sen wasn't who I thought he was, and neither is

Prince Raja Prasad. He's offering his arm and asking me to walk.

"Where will we go?" I gaze at drab lawns struggling up between driveways, the houses so dark and still, it's hard to believe anyone lives in them.

"I thought we might try the beach."

Twenty-four

Ocean Beach is a wide strip of golden sand imprinted with the tire tracks of off-road vehicles. A couple walks in the distance with a dog that zigzags along the water's edge. Gulls soar overhead, and whitecaps churn in a dance against the hazy sky.

Raja takes off his shoes and socks, tucks the socks into the shoes, and carries them. I follow suit. The sand squishes between my toes, and I dig my feet in as I rush to keep up with his strides.

"I've been out here so many times, but I've never walked on this beach," I say.

"We often miss what's right in front of us."

It sounds like a quote from some book, but it's true. I examine his profile, the breeze pushing back his hair, the lines of his face rugged against the foggy sky. I want to ask how he got the scar.

We wade in ankle-deep water, white foam rushing over our feet. He steps over a charred driftwood log floating soggy in the surf. My feet are going numb, so I move up to the dry sand.

"You intrigue me." He gazes at me as if I'm a new species of starfish. "You live alone. You're unmarried."

"Lots of single women live perfectly normal lives here in America." My ears heat up. My face is probably already red and scoured by the wind.

"Is your life perfectly normal? Or perhaps your life is too normal. You forget to walk on beaches."

"I'm busy."

"And you're cold. Come on, let's run." He breaks into a smooth trot, and I follow, running and running until we both collapse, gasping for breath.

Raja sits in the sand and squints out to sea. "This coast reminds me of Puri."

"I've been there once. On the Bay of Bengal. My family stayed there when I was a kid."

"We have a vacation home there, a house with steps right down to the beach. I go there to think, to listen to the sea.

The beach stretches for miles, and the sand is white and hot."

"Sounds lovely."

"You must come. You're welcome to stay at our home."

"Wow—are you serious? Thanks. I'm honored." I'm tongue-tied. Why does a prince want me to visit his vacation home? Maybe it's customary to invite everybody. Horror—maybe he doesn't expect me to *accept* the invitation. "I couldn't, though. I mean, it's expensive to fly to India, and I'm not sure I can take more time off. You know—"

"You'll love the ocean there. I remember when I was a boy lying in bed beneath the mosquito net and listening to the surf."

"It's nice to have a place to go. When things get crazy, I mean."

"I watch the fishermen take to sea in their wooden canoes. Somehow, they manage to ride the rogue waves, but it's a dangerous business. They often drown. I swim there anyway. Do you ever swim?"

"In southern California. Not here. It's too cold, and there are riptides—"

"I thought you liked swimming out far." He leaps to his feet, grabs my hand, and yanks me toward the water.

"What are you doing? You're crazy!"

"It'll wake you up." He heads straight for the sea, grabs me around the waist, and lifts me easily in his arms as he wades into the surf, the freezing spray, and then we both go down. I come up gasping. He dunks me again, and I'm shivering.

"I'm wide awake now," I gasp, my soaked clothes clinging to my skin.

He rides a shallow wave. "You only live once!"

"We'll get hypothermia! What if the current pulls us out? There's no lifeguard." But I flop on my belly, teeth chattering, and bodysurf in. He takes my hand again. I feel like Deborah Kerr in *From Here to Eternity.*

The water warms around me, and then euphoria washes over me, or maybe I'm drowning. That must be it. I hear you experience euphoria right before losing consciousness. I float for a minute, hyper-aware of the sea. "Do you think there might be sharks too?"

"If there are, we'll ride with them." I feel his powerful arms around my thighs, drawing me under. Someone's screaming, then I realize it's me. I'm screaming with laughter, and then he throws me in the air again, and I hit the water with a great splash. Not that I'm heavy or anything.

When Raja stands, I see the muscular outline of his body beneath his clothes, and I realize how much bigger he is than me, and a thrill rushes through me, and then I realize that if I can see his whole body, he must be able to see mine too. Too late to duck.

His gaze sweeps from my knees to my head, and I dip beneath the water, crossing my arms over my chest.

He grabs my arm. "Your lips are blue. Let's get out."

We run back to the car, our clothes slapping our bodies, our ankles covered in sand. We're sea creatures trying to shuffle along on land.

"I should go home and change clothes," I say.

Raja puts his hand over mine. "Come to my hotel. It's closer. They have laundry service."

Twenty-five

At the Hilton, Raja ushers me into the bedroom, says he'll be right back, and disappears into the separate living room, complete with wet bar and fireplace.

I stand shivering, clasping my hands in front of me, my clothes dripping on the carpet. Okay, breathe. It's just a hotel room in pale blue, with no hint at Raja's inner self except the faint scent of his spicy, exotic aftershave.

I can't help glancing sidelong at the bed. King-sized hotel mattress covered with a shiny blue bedspread. What did I expect? An Indian brass bed with elephant-head knobs and a silk canopy? A harem of scantily clad women waving massive palm frond fans, waiting for their master to return?

I try not to picture Raja Prasad sleeping in the bed. Does he lie on his side or sprawled on his back? Does he snore? Does he even sleep? Maybe he has wild sex every night with a different woman. If so, what kind of women? Does he think I'm going be one of them? Maybe, but right now my teeth chatter and my lips are numb. Some women like cold. Ice cubes and all that. I prefer warmth to hypothermia.

There's a book on the nightstand, and a tumbler on a coaster with what looks like a shot of whisky in the bottom of the glass. I imagine his Adam's apple moving up and down as he gulps the whisky. He'll wince as the sharp alcohol burns his throat. Sexy.

My teeth chatter, and my fingers are numb. He's rooting around in the entryway closet. What's he doing in there? I focus on the book: *India: An Area of Darkness*. There's a closed suitcase on an armchair, a laptop computer on a desk. A suit jacket hangs over the armchair.

"Please, have a shower," Raja says behind me, making me jump. He hands me a folded white robe. "You'll find clean towels in the bathroom." He points.

"What about you?"

"There's another bathroom."

Another one? Of course. I rush into the bathroom, lock the door, and peel off my clothes. Goose bumps cover my body. I can't stop shaking, but when I catch a glimpse of myself in the mirror, I'm smiling and my eyes shine. Am I feverish? Maybe I'm catching pneumonia.

I glance into the tile shower. Two showerheads. *Come in here with me, Raja. Keep me warm,* I'm thinking, but he's not going to hop into the shower with some Americanized pretend-Indian woman who resembles seaweed. I don't live with my parents. I rarely follow their advice. I can't wear virgin white at my wedding, but then, nobody wears white at Indian weddings. In India, white is the color of mourning.

I spend way too long beneath the delicious heat of the shower. I use the sandalwood soap and shave my legs with Raja's razor. I lather Mysore shampoo into my hair until I smell like a giant coconut. I imagine Raja naked in the other bathroom. Is he showering in there? Does he have extra soap, razors, and shampoo? Is he thinking of me naked in here? Does he wish he could be in here with me? I nearly drive myself crazy fantasizing, and then I realize my imaginary man is absent again.

When I emerge from the shower, I feel I've shared a new intimacy with Raja Prasad. Today I've seen an impulsive side of him. He dragged me into freezing surf, then walked waterlogged through the Hilton lobby. He didn't care that people stared, that we left puddles in our wake. Strange for a man obsessed with appearances.

I battle my reflection in the mirror, tell myself I'm here to get dry and warm, but I can't help noticing his Sonicare toothbrush, a match to mine.

"Are you all right?" he says outside the door. "Do you need another robe?"

"No. Thanks! I'm just coming out." I throw on the robe, tie the sash. The robe goes down to my ankles and the sleeves flop over my hands. Call me Shirley Temple in men's clothing.

He's whistling a Hindi tune in the living room, where I find a fake fire crackling in the hearth. He's wearing jeans and a gray turtleneck sweater, and I could swear he belongs in the Indian version of the L. L. Bean catalog.

"Your clothes are in the laundry," he says. "Would you like to borrow mine?"

I go back to the bedroom and pull on a pair of jeans that nearly fall off my waist, tie them with a belt and roll the bottoms up several times, then pull on a T-shirt that falls past my knees, tuck it in, and tug a thick black woolen sweater over it. I'm ready to walk the runway at a celebrity fashion show. The Woman Swimming in Raja Prasad's clothes.

When I return to the living area, Raja grins, amusement in his eyes. He hands me a glass of sherry. "To warm you up. Sit." He points to the plush couch, and I curl up on it, happy to feel the heat of the fake fire on my skin.

I sip the sherry and savor the liquid rushing down my throat.

He sits beside me. "If Dev is to meet Kali, it must be soon. I'm traveling again next Saturday."

My heart drops, then plummets through the earth, and I scold it for being so fickle, for leaving behind my imaginary man tonight. I need my phantom fiancé, because I can't fall for Raja. He's nearly engaged. We rolled through the surf together, nothing more.

He drapes an arm over my shoulders. My heartbeat picks up. I'm aware of his size, his strength. But of course, he's leaving. Just as men always leave. Just as Nathu left. Okay, Nathu died, but that's a form of leaving.

I cross my arms over my chest and babble about anything and everything. Stupid things, like the way waxed dental floss leaves a residue on your teeth, so you should use unwaxed floss. He lets me talk, watches my lips move.

"I don't want to leave," he says, leaning close. The heat rises from his skin. I reach for my imaginary man, but he falls off a cliff and disappears.

Twenty-six

*T*he next morning I'm in yoga class, stuck in the downward-facing dog position. The blood rushes to my head. Inhale, exhale. Six A.M. is too early for exercise.

"It's all about the breathing," the instructor says over the monotonous drone of meditative music. She's a rubber-bodied brunette who twists herself into a variety of pretzel shapes to make us all envious.

"So Raja took you to his suite?" Donna whispers beside me. "Tell, tell."

"I've never known a guy who would swim in Ocean Beach with all the riptides! Maybe he has a death wish."

"He loves life. He's spontaneous," Donna says.

"Or he had a momentary lapse of common sense."

"A lapse that extends to washing your clothes and offering you sherry?"

"You're right. He was romantic. And he runs orphanages to help little girls. I don't get it. He's so proper. He dresses in expensive, tailored suits and wants everything perfect. He wants the perfect wife for his brother, and probably for himself too. But there's a caring, wild man underneath all that propriety."

At the instructor's command, we step forward and rise into mountain stance.

"Sounds like a dream man to me. So you had caring, wild sex?" Donna whispers.

"Ha! I wish we had. He let slip a small fact. He's practically engaged."

We all lunge forward into warrior pose, front leg bent at the knee, back leg extended.

"What does that mean? Engagements are reversible. You have to get the scoop from him."

"It's none of my business. It was wrong of me to go to his hotel room."

"Oh, wrong of you! Now you have a conscience? You went anyway. For a reason. There's always a reason."

"I got caught up in his—"

"—to-die-for good looks and charm? That'd be enough for me."

As we unwind through the relaxation poses, I imagine Raja Prasad as a wild man in Puri, at his home by the sea. I picture him jumping into the wooden boats and floating out with the fishermen. Does he perform religious ablutions in the morning? Does he chant his prayers? Does he brush his teeth three times a day?

After class, in the gym shower, I close my eyes and juxtapose his image against every guy I've dated. Dr. Dilip Dutta, Patrick Malloy, Pramit Lall. They shrink into tiny hobbits, and Raja grows into King Aragorn, handsome and noble.

I towel off and dress in jeans and a sweater. There has to be a comparable man. I had fun taking windsurfing lessons with a freckled sailor. We laughed and hiked and dined together, until I discovered he was laughing and hiking and dining with two other women, one Korean, one African-American. His Rainbow Coalition.

Raja would never do such a thing. He's loyal to his mother, his brother, his life in India. He'll be loyal to his wife, too.

Back at my apartment, I'm alone and restless. I forsake my usual cup of tea and make coffee instead. Why not take a risk, go out on a limb? The hot liquid tastes bitter, so I douse it with sugar and the organic milk that Harry left behind.

I sit at the breakfast nook to read the newspaper, but I stare out the window instead, at the Chinese women, their long hair pulled back into shiny, black buns, strolling up the sidewalk, carrying bags of produce home from Chinatown shops. Then a knock comes on the door.

My heartbeat races. Oh, God, oh, God, it's him. No, it must be a solicitor. But there's a big sign downstairs: NO SOLICITORS. It's Kali, Donna, Harry.

On the way to the door, I nearly kill myself with anticipation. I glance at my reflection in the hall mirror. I look like an Indian Medusa. I run my fingers through my hair.

Another knock.

"Coming, coming!" I peer through the peephole. Oh, God, again. Raja stands in the hallway clad in black turtleneck and jeans.

He looks rested, his hair neat.

I step back to get my bearings. Breathe in, breathe out. He was a dream, but now he's not, or maybe I'm still dreaming. Maybe this is a dream within a dream within a dream. Where's my imaginary man when I need him?

I open the door. "Raja! I wasn't expecting you."

"Breakfast?"

"I'll be just a minute."

"I'll wait downstairs."

I pull on my shoes, my heart racing. It's been a long time since I felt this way. *Flustered.* I'm downstairs in record time.

"You look beautiful," he says.

Warmth travels up through my insides and radiates along my limbs. He's attracted to me. Me, the Indian-American woman with frizzy hair. A silly smile spreads across my face. "Thanks. You look pretty good yourself."

He nods, as if women say this to him every day. Then we're out on the street, walking together as if we've always walked this way. The Chinese women smile as they pass, their arms laden with bags of bok choi and bamboo shoots.

My heart beats fast, and the colors of morning seem brighter. I'm filled with well-being. Our strides fit together perfectly. He doesn't walk too fast for me today.

We talk about the landscapes we pass, the people, the sky, the city. I'm floating, living in the moment for the first time in two years.

At Milton's Diner, we find a window booth. The restaurant is abuzz with an eclectic mix of San Franciscans, all fuzzy and fresh in the morning. I order the tofu scramble with onions, and Raja orders an omelet. After breakfast, we drive south, away from the city. The farther we go, the more relaxed the lines of his face become. We park at Shoreline Park, beneath a slightly pink, smoggy sky.

"How did you know the way here?" I ask.

He reaches over me, his arm brushing my leg, and opens the glove compartment. "Maps."

I barely breathe with him so close, and he pulls out a pair of binoculars. "What are you going to use those for?"

"Bird-watching."

Another surprise. We walk in silence on the path along the canal, and I fall into step beside him.

He points at pelicans, their shapes gangly and prehistoric as they guzzle fish. "White pelicans, very rare. And there, a snowy egret. They wear golden slippers."

"So they do! Amazing." I hand back the binoculars. "You're an astronomer *and* a naturalist."

He fixes me with a studied gaze. "I'm interested in many things, including you. I was watching you at Durga's wedding."

I blush, the heat creeping from my ears up to the roots of my hair.

We drive to Berkeley, wander through Urban Outfitters, Bancroft Clothing Company. We order *samosas* at Vik's Chaat House and eat them with our hands, licking the curry sauce from our fingers. We browse through Serendipity Books, and meet at the entrance at precisely the same time with books in our arms.

We drive back to Palo Alto, stop at the Stanford Museum. The air is cool and controlled inside, bringing goose bumps to my skin, or maybe the goose bumps are from Raja's proximity. I feel small and fragile around him. I picture my imaginary man pacing in the apartment, flicking the TV channels.

We wander past the Rodin exhibits; marvel at a massive black cast of *The Thinker;* stare at Degas sculptures found in his studio after his death, at Andy Warhol's piles of Brillo pad boxes constructed from wood and paint, and a Japanese tea set from the eighteenth century. We find an Egyptian mummy from two thousand years ago. The hieroglyphics call her "Chantress of the Sun."

"The coffin is so small." I press my nose to the glass display case. "Like she was a child."

Raja comes up behind me, his chest against my back as he leans over me, so close, to see the mummy. Across two thousand years, Chantress of the Sun is casting a spell on us.

Twenty-seven

We have afternoon tea at C'est Café and watch people. At a table under an umbrella, I take in university life—Calvin Klein's Obsession perfume, cigarettes, nose rings, and skimpy, midriff-baring outfits.

"Tell me about your fiancée," I say.

He chokes on his tea. "My fiancée?"

"What's her name." I can afford to watch him through sunglasses. He can't see the expression on my face. "I mean, should you even be out with me?"

He clears his throat and takes another sip of tea. "Her name is Sayantoni. She's a princess."

A princess. The word cuts through me. She must be beautiful. I run my finger around the rim of my teacup. I want him to say he's not really engaged. It was all a rumor. Now his woman has a name.

"What's she like?"

"I don't know her well. My father knew her father."

"But you've gone out with her."

"I've met her."

"You're with family when you see her?"

"Yes. Her parents arrange the meetings."

"And you go along."

He sits back, his face shaded by the umbrella. "I respect my mother's wishes. She wants to see me happy."

"If you don't know this woman, how do you know you'll be happy with her?"

He gulps his coffee. "We come from similar backgrounds. She understands what's required."

There he goes again, describing a Stepford Wife. The ghost princess drives a wedge between us. "Was she promised to you, like a child bride?"

He laughs. "Of course not. You know the Brahmo Samaj don't believe in child brides."

"But you agreed to the match."

"Not yet, although her family would like my response soon."

"Oh," I say faintly. "Do you . . . know what you'll do?"

"I haven't decided. Although . . . she comes from a good family."

I'm from a good family too. "Are you in love with her?"

He breaks into a startled smile. "You are direct."

"Well, are you?"

"Love takes time. It's learned."

"So you're not in love with her . . . yet. But you think you might be in love with her, someday?"

"Perhaps." He grins. I'm amusing him.

"You don't believe in love at first sight?"

"Perhaps, but such was not the case with her."

"Is she pretty?"

"Ah, well." He looks off down the sidewalk. He has to think about it?

"I mean, she's a princess, right? Does she look like a princess?"

"In a traditional way." He shifts in his seat. "Anyway, it's of no consequence. She's willing to become a good wife. That's what matters."

"To take care of your family."

"She's very respectful. Well educated, well read—"

"A perfect ornament for your palace." Oops, what did I just say?

He doesn't answer, and I don't blame him.

"Sorry." Jealousy claws at my gut. "What would she think if she knew you were with me?"

"Lina—" He leans in close. His breath warms my cheek.

"Did you know I had a fiancé once? He died two years ago."

"I'm sorry—" He touches my chin, turns my face toward him.

"Yeah, well. I think he may not have been exactly faithful."

"Then he was the wrong man for you." He angles his face to kiss me, softly at first, and then his lips are demanding and direct. The kiss radiates through my body. His face is flushed, his eyes half-lidded.

I pull away and straighten up, my breathing shallow and quick. I can't compete with an Indian princess.

Twenty-eight

_H_arry and Jonathan hold their commitment ceremony outside at Bear Valley, at the Point Reyes National Seashore. Hills of pink and yellow wildflowers roll away to the edge of the forest. An ocean breeze wafts through the crowd. I stand in a semicircle with the maids of honor in blue dresses and sandals.

Harry and Jon stand on a platform in front of the priest. They both look stunning in tuxedoes, their hair slicked back. A bright thread of love shimmers between them, connecting their hearts.

A lump lodges in my throat. I hate weddings. I'm not the

type to be hitched, at least, not anymore, and I can't understand why I get emotional at these shindigs.

People of all persuasions are here. Most of gay San Francisco must've shown up—the city is missing half its population. I didn't know Harry and Jon were so popular. The priest recites the commitment vows, and the two men respond with relish.

". . . in sickness and in health, until death do you part . . ."

I blink back tears. I imagine Raja Prasad marrying his princess. Will he have a typical Brahmo Samaj wedding? Why did he bother kissing a dark, thin, neurotic, single American woman who can't cook Bengali food?

He thinks I'm honest and forthright, but I'm a fraud.

When the ceremony ends, Harry and Jon kiss, and Jon lifts Harry off his feet. They throw the birdseed into the air, and Harry throws a bouquet. Donna catches it.

"You're next!" I hug her.

"No, you are." She mouths *Raja Prasad.*

I shake my head. "Just business. I'm introducing his brother to my sister."

"There, see? Two brothers will marry two sisters."

"No chance." I ask Donna to come with me for moral support.

"I get to meet the fab Dev? Of course."

"You're a doll, Donna. I owe you my life." I make my way to Harry and Jon and embrace them both.

Harry's face glows with happiness. "I can't wait to get out of this place. Paris, here we come!"

"Take me with you?"

"Any time, honey." But I don't figure into his plans. He's smiling into his future with Jonathan.

Then the crowd moves in, hugging and shaking hands, and I drift away from the throng. A bubble of isolation surrounds me. I watch couples holding hands, some mothers wearing T-shirts, "Proud Parent of a Gay," kids running around.

I walk away from the group, down the path to the sea.

Twenty-nine

When I arrive at Madras Cuisine, Raja, Dev, and Kali are already seated in a booth. No sign of Donna. Kali's in a silk blouse buttoned to her neck. Her hair twists up into an Audrey Hepburn *Breakfast at Tiffany's* style. She's desperate to impress Raja, the Important Elder Brother.

Dev stands and kisses the back of my hand. He's slightly shorter than Raja, with narrower shoulders and a wider face, but there's no mistaking the Prasad features and charm. We make the introductions. Our stiff formality could starch all the red cloth napkins in the restaurant.

Kali's doing the demure, looking-down thing. I try not to

roll my eyes as I take a seat next to Raja. His elbow brushes mine.

Dev's gaze pierces me. I wonder if he's searching for similarities between Kali and me. He pours Heineken into a glass, spilling a drop on the white tablecloth.

I glance from Dev to Kali and back. No shimmering thread connects them, no body language that hints at the two becoming lovers. Doesn't matter, I tell myself, if Kali says they have cross-mojonation.

Dev lifts his glass. "Here's to making perfect matches." His tone is acid, but we raise our glasses. Kali leaves an imprint of red lipstick on hers.

We talk, throwing formal questions and answers like hot potatoes. What does Dev do? What are Kali's interests? What does she hope to accomplish in life, and what's she looking for in a husband? She responds in a patient, polite tone, like a programmed robot. Although she loves her job at *City Chic*, she really wants to settle down and raise children.

"—Dev is finishing his MBA, and then he will return to work in the family business," Raja says.

"Maybe I prefer to remain here," Dev says.

Raja shoots him a look. An invisible storm rages between brothers. I have an urge to run for shelter.

Kali stares down at the napkin in her lap.

Where's Donna when I need her? I check my cell phone. No message, so we order without her. I barely notice the meal, a combination of South Indian *masala dhosas*—crepes with curried potato and vegetables inside—dipped in a coconut or hot tomato curry sauce. The conversation swirls as I watch Dev, who never once looks at Kali. He keeps casting me questioning glances.

"When would you like to get married?" Kali asks Dev.

"Not too soon. I came tonight mainly out of obligation to my family."

Kali's face reddens.

I twist the cloth napkin in my lap. At least he's honest.

Raja clears his throat, the skin around his lips turning pale. "His auspicious wedding date falls in five months."

Kali chokes on a sip of water.

I'm going to throw up. I stand, place my napkin carefully on the table. "Will you excuse me a moment?" I dash to the bathroom, a small green-tiled room with a noisy fan and the smell of Lysol disinfectant. My mind whirls, my brain dampened by sulfites from the wine. Poor Kali.

I set up this meeting. Maybe there's still a chance to save the evening, but how? Suggest Kali and Dev take a drive together? Does Dev have any real interest in her?

I splash cold water on my face, pat my hair, and take deep breaths. I step into the hall and bump into Dev. His cologne is sharper than his brother's is, and there's a hint of alcohol on his breath.

He stands back, blocking the hallway. "Are you all right?"

"Peachy keen." My trademark words.

"I apologize for the remark I made to your sister. I like her. She's lovely, but I need time to consider my future. I have many options, and marriage is a big step."

"No rush. Take your time." I think of the missing silver threads.

He steps back. "I hope Kali doesn't find me rude."

"She thinks she's falling in love with you. She doesn't know what she really wants." I squeeze past Dev, and my legs wobble all the way back to the booth. Plates of dessert cover the table. I try a spoonful of coconut *burfi*, made from coconut and cashews and cardamom, and crunch down on the sickly sweetness.

Dev comes back and sits down, and then Donna rushes in, a pale goddess in a white dress. "So sorry I'm late! Emergency at home. Long story. Lina, you have permission to kill me. What did I miss? Raja, great to see you again. Kali, you look beautiful. And you must be Dev—"

He takes her hand. She gazes up at him, and she and Dev take off to a distant planet. A translucent silver thread shimmers between them.

Thirty

Harry and Jonathan have been staying with me for two days. Their furniture is bobbing across the Atlantic Ocean on a ship bound for Europe. Harry folds laundry on my couch, and I'm plucking my eyebrows when the doorbell rings. I put down the tweezers and mirror and stare at the door, then at Harry. He stares at me. Jonathan is whistling "I Can See Clearly Now" in the shower.

"See who it is," I whisper.

Harry carries a folded undershirt to the door and squints through the peephole. "It's him!"

"Him? Him who?"

"Him."

"Oh, no!" I screech. "He's not here. He's in New York."

"Then it must be his evil twin."

"Don't you open that door." I jump to my feet and gather the laundry from the couch. The cold morning leaps into my bones. Folded clothes slip from my arms and fall on the floor. The doorbell rings again, more insistently this time.

"You're just a friend visiting," I say as I pick up a pile of briefs from the chair. "Better yet, hide in the bedroom, and I'll get it."

Harry is already opening the door. I'll kill him.

Raja Prasad storms in. I'm standing in the middle of the living room in my sweats, a folded pile of Jonathan's sexy Jockeys in my arms. "It's not what you think."

"Your engagement is not what I think?" Raja glances at me, at the pile, at Harry, and then back at me. "Word gets around. Did you think I wouldn't find out?"

How could I have expected people to keep their mouths shut? "Oh, Raja. I'm not really engaged!"

"Oh, really? I returned early, stopped by your office, and Donna said you'd left. I read the postcards. Every one of them. I won't ask why you didn't tell me."

"Those postcards were fakes!"

Harry reaches out to shake Raja's hand. "I wrote them, of course. Pleased to meet you. I've heard so much about you. All good."

Raja shakes his hand, but his face is hard. "I'd heard nothing about you, until recently. Seems all of India knows, but I've been out of the loop."

"I apologize." Harry turns to me. "Lina will come clean, won't she? She'll tell you everything."

Baba will crumble into dust. Ma will sequester herself until the end of time. Kiki will marry me to Pee-wee. "It's complicated," I say.

Raja turns to Harry. "You must be her fiancé, the man who travels incessantly."

"I do travel quite a bit." Harry winks at me.

"I'm sorry I didn't tell you," I say to Raja. "It's a long story. It's about my parents, and my auntie Kiki. They so desperately want me to settle down, marry, and have kids."

Raja turns to Harry. "Do you not realize how difficult your absence has been for her?"

"She was all broken up," Harry says.

What's going on?

"How can you take this so lightly?" Raja says. "How could you leave her behind for so many months? If you're to be a good husband, you'll have to stay with her. It is unacceptable to leave her alone."

"Whoa. You have it all wrong. This lecture isn't meant for me." Harry holds up his hands.

"You must accept responsibility for your actions."

Jonathan saunters out of the bedroom, biceps flexing, only

a towel wrapped around his waist. His dark hair is still wet and matted against his neck. "Lina, have you seen my underwear?"

"Here." I hold out the pile in my arms.

Raja's face reddens, confusion in his eyes.

"Raja, this is Jonathan." My mouth goes dry. I feel the ice creeping through the apartment.

"I thought your fiancé's name was also Raja," Raja says.

Jonathan gives Raja an appraising look. "You're the only Raja we know, and I'm very pleased to meet you," he says, then goes to Harry and plants a kiss on his lips. Jonathan says, "I took a great shower, I wish you could've joined me," to Harry, and then a strange light of understanding comes to Raja's eyes. His face transforms into an expression of dismay, surprise, and a myriad of other emotions. I know his thoughts. *How could you deceive me, Lina Ray?*

I find my legs, drop the underwear, and run to him. I grab his hands, but he yanks them away and strides for the door. I'm babbling. "Let me explain. It's a big hoax. In India, there was so much pressure. I made up someone."

He stops with his hand on the doorknob. "Harry. His name is Harry. Not Raja?"

"No, I . . . used your name. The first name that came into my head. Please, I'm sorry." I follow him out the door and down the stairs as I try to explain, my words like boomerangs hitting me in the face. Outside on the curb, he hails a taxi, and then he's gone.

Thirty-one

At work, I remove the postcards from Harry and throw them into the recycling bin. Then I sit at my desk and watch morning brighten across Chinatown. The sun hangs at the wrong angle in the sky. One minute I shiver, and the next minute the sweat droplets pop out on my forehead. The thermostat must be on the blink, or maybe my internal climate control has gone bonkers. I'm going through early menopause. Yes, that's it. The hot flashes are starting, and I haven't even had a chance to mate. What is it about love?

Maybe chemistry. Is that what love comes down to? Beakers and steaming liquids and elements and chemical reactions and Bunsen burners? Is that what Raja and I were? Two Bunsen burners passing in the night?

My voice-mail light blinks. I press through the messages. Mrs. Mukerjee demands to know why I set up her daughter with a lech who could be her great-grandfather.

"Grandfather, not great," I mumble, jotting down the message. I forgot to look at the man's age. The Mukerjees have an appointment here later this morning.

I listen for Raja Prasad's message, but it never comes. Why would he call? I tried phoning his hotel, but he'd checked out.

So what? To be with him, I would have to leave my whole life behind. I couldn't jog in shorts in India, could I? I'd have to wear heavy long pants that flap against my legs. I'd trip over them and fall on the dirty ground and get heatstroke or cholera or typhoid fever. Everyone would look at me and wonder whether I was a wandering ascetic rolling across India, occasionally falling in the ditch. I would have to cook. What would happen to my morning tea and newspaper?

It's best that Raja doesn't want me.

At nine, my first customer waltzes in, a wispy Indian, former Bollywood actress whose rich husband left her for a younger woman. She's got a new hot number on her arm, a blond god probably ten years her junior. She wanted a non-Indian stud, and she got one. A diamond ring glints on her finger, the rock almost heavy enough to topple her over.

"I'd like you to meet my fiancé, John," she says.

"Pleased to meet you. Glad I could help." I give them both a wide smile. I don't remember him.

"I didn't meet him through you," she says coldly. "In fact, I came to tell you that you messed up."

I glance at her file. My vision blurs as I read the cramped handwriting. She wanted a young, rich, generous husband. "I didn't notice—"

"No, you didn't, that's the problem. He took me to the Outback Steakhouse. The man was a Neanderthal. A carnivore. Tearing the meat from the bones. He would be a cannibal given the chance."

"Given the chance," her boy toy echoes. He gives her a loving look.

"I nearly threw up," she says.

"She nearly threw up," he says.

I nearly throw up. "I'm sorry."

"You'd better be. I want my money back."

After I return her fee, she and her beau stalk out, and at ten o'clock Mr. Sen bursts into my office, his suit askew, as if he got dressed in REM sleep with his brain on backward. Or maybe he actually looks fine and *my* brain is on backward.

I wonder how I messed up this time. Everything I touch turns to dirt, or at least catches a serious case of dust bunnies. Even the office is disheveled. "Have a seat, Mr. Sen. How can I help you?"

"I don't want to sit."

I should be worried. Or regretful. I should beg his forgiveness and give him a refund, but I gaze at the windowsill where the crumpled rose petals are scattered. I imbued them with the sentiment of a man who never existed. Can't Mr. Sen see I'm mourning a lost love? The roses are dead, and I'm tired, but I prop my eyes open with phantom toothpicks. My mouth does overtime with this smiling business. What does a smile mean, anyway? It's all in the eyes.

He paces, his suit threatening to slip off his narrow frame. I'll soon have a naked Mr. Sen in my office, or at least a Mr. Sen in his underwear, a prospect that should horrify me, but I'm numb.

"Miss Chatterjee didn't want me, so I went on another date. It was all wrong."

"I'm so sorry." I can't fix what I've broken. I try to imagine shimmering silver filaments connecting Mr. Sen to a woman I picked for him, but I see nothing.

"That, that woman you suggested. I had dinner with her." He points at the file folder on my desk, as if it's Pandora's Box. *That woman.*

"And how did it go?"

"How did it go? You want to know how it went?" He strides to the window, stares out as if he wants to fling himself to the pavement. "To begin with, she's very dark. The photograph must've been doctored, made to look as if she's fair-skinned."

191

"I thought she was pretty." I look at my own arms, the skin tanned from jogs in the sun.

He tugs at his wrinkled collar. "Pretty, yes, but what's on the inside matters most, nah? She was nice on the inside, of course, but then—" He takes a deep breath. "We were discussing this and that, the cities of our youth, our parents—"

"Sounds as though you got along well."

He laughs, a thin whistle through his nose. "Hah, got along well. I'll say. I was even imagining our families meeting, the wedding, and finally settling down to proper married life."

"A good thing to imagine." The breeze lifts a few dry rose petals and sends them sailing to the carpet.

"And then I discover—" His face screws up into a disgusted expression. "That she's a Muslim." He spits the word as if it's a rotten grape.

"How could I not have spotted this in the file?"

"Oh, Shiva." He looks to the ceiling, as if the Hindu gods might hear him, except they aren't in heaven, they're all around us in parallel worlds they've created for their own amusement.

"I'm so sorry," I say. "Chalk it up to an unfortunate mistake." My whole life is an unfortunate mistake. An unfortunate series of mistakes. Call me Lina Ray, the Unfortunate Serial Mistake.

"It's more than a mistake." He shakes his head, keeps

shaking it like a dog trying to get dry. "My grandparents fought Muslims during partition in 1948. I'm past all that, nah? I know Muslims. I have Muslim friends. I respect the religion, but I'm not a Muslim. I will never be a Muslim. I will never worship Allah, never kneel or fast for Ramadan. But there I was, sharing a meal in public, in a restaurant with a Muslim, and I actually considered marrying her, because of you!"

Everything happens because of me. I'm convinced of this now, more than ever. The earth must wobble on its axis because of me. Whales beach themselves because of me. Auntie will be disappointed and heartsick because of me.

I apologize profusely. Sorry, Please Forgive Me. Mr. Sen is humiliated, mortified.

I've royally screwed up everything.

Thirty-two

I'm late leaving town for Baba's birthday party, and it's my imaginary man's fault. He argues with me all morning, begs me to stay, but I grit my teeth and pack my duffel bag, letting him rant.

Let me ride in your luggage.

"There's no room for you, now that you're huge and muscular. You're looking too much like Raja Prasad, and he doesn't want me." I stuff panties, bras, books, jeans, and T-shirts into the bag.

What will you tell Auntie Kiki?

I bite my lip. He always asks the difficult questions.

My whole life has collapsed beneath the weight of my lies, but I'm going to dig my way out. "I'm telling everyone the truth today. It's time to stop the charade. They'll have to believe me this time." I slump on the bed next to my duffel bag, the new V. S. Naipaul book of essays heavy in my lap. Baba will like this book. Naipaul has a finger on the pulse of the Indian exile. I, on the other hand, don't have much of a pulse. I'm the walking dead.

You're in love with Raja Prasad. Go after him.

"I had my chance. Now he hates me, with good reason. I'm a fake. I should be made of plastic, modeling swimwear in JCPenney. Except I'm too dark and not shaped right."

Don't denigrate yourself that way. You're beautiful.

"At least an imaginary person thinks so." My deranged laughter echoes through the apartment. "There's zero chance that Raja and I could be together. I have to face reality. He'll go back to India and marry the princess. She probably speaks a million languages. I bet she can feel a pea under fifty mattresses."

Stop talking nonsense. Stay with me.

"I can't." For the first time, I don't want my imaginary man around. I'm turning into one of those crazy people on Telegraph Avenue in Berkeley, gesturing to a nonexistent companion and mumbling to myself. I snap my fingers, but he doesn't entirely disappear. He fades in and out, his face changing into Raja and then blanking out, then changing back. It's like when you try to blow out all the candles on a birthday cake, but a few stubborn flames continue to flicker, mocking you.

"I have to get rid of you."

His eyes widen in horror. *So that's why I've been a bit dizzy lately.*

"You have to go. Scram, skedaddle."

Where will I go? I have no home. This is my home.

"Fly away and live in someone else's imagination."

He follows me to the dressing table. I grab Star Galaxy and tuck the stone into my handbag. I need to keep it close, the only thing I have left of Raja Prasad. I slide the golden serpent bangle onto my wrist and pin the golden brooch to my shirt.

Outside, the chilly air sinks into my bones. Clean air, free of deception. I wonder what Raja's doing right now. Having tea with the princess? Dinner with his mother? Traipsing into the jungle? It's late in India. He's probably in bed.

I still taste his lips on mine. I turn, and my imaginary man is gone. All I see are patterns and shadows on the wall, and suddenly I want to reach my parents' house as quickly as I can, just to be with people.

Seven hours later, I park on the curb. Baba's birthday party is in full swing. I see lights through the windows and the silhouettes of people talking and holding wineglasses. Cars clutter the driveway and the street, some parked halfway on the grass. I pull down the visor mirror, wipe the sweat from my face. My heart hammers. The house bursts with guests, and I sense Auntie Kiki's presence. She glares at me from every window, her piercing eye disapproving of my shiny face, tangled hair, and dirty silver Honda. So many times on the drive down, I wanted to pull a one-eighty and race home, but the monotony of the highway past King City lulled me into a hopeful stupor. Maybe it won't matter if my fiancé isn't here. Maybe Baba's birthday party will be all about Baba, and everyone will forget the old-maid daughter hiding in the shadows.

I've let everyone down. Kali, Raja, my parents, myself. I shouldn't be here, but I get out of the car, walk up the driveway, ring the doorbell, open the door, and call out into the smell of frying curry and onion, the sound of laughter from the kitchen. Auntie Kiki's voice sends a chill of apprehension down my spine. She can outtalk anyone, shoot her mouth off with perfect, deadly aim.

Ma comes rushing down the hall. "I was worried about you. I thought you'd had an accident." She peers past me toward the car, straining her eyes in the darkness.

"I'm fine, Ma. I got a late start."

"*Acha.* You're here now. Hurry and freshen up." The evening bears down, strangling me.

"I have to talk to you and Baba."

"Later—the guests are waiting." Ma's scent of gardenia lotion comforts me. The familiar sounds of the kettle clanging on the stove, the cabinets swinging open and shut, laughter and conversation, fill me with a calming sense of home. I wish I were a child again, when lies were simple. You came clean, got a talking-to, and got on with growing up. Now I'm grown, and my lies may never untangle themselves.

"I have to do it now, Ma. I have an announcement—"

"Eat first. You must be famished. We've made a feast. We've been anticipating this moment for weeks." She pulls me inside, and I drop my duffel bag by the stairs.

"It's been a long drive. How's Baba?"

"He's been in quite a buoyant mood today. You know why."

Oh, no—this will be harder than I thought.

Durga bounces in from the back room. She's a radiant Olympic champion, biceps flexing as she lifts her red sari. "Lina, omigod! I'm so happy you're finally here!" We hug, and she pulls back, her face aglow. "Hurry—we're all waiting."

"They may be waiting forever." Nobody's asking about my fiancé. Maybe they expect me to pull him from a hat.

Durga gives me a puzzled look, then forges on. "I can't wait to tell you about our disastrous honeymoon in Goa. Rained the entire time. Our hut leaked, and the toilet overflowed. We had such fun anyway. I miss Amit *so* much. He's still back in Delhi visiting an uncle. I'm counting down. Only five days, six hours, and thirty-seven minutes until he returns."

"You were always good with numbers." If I count down

the days until I see Raja again, I'll be counting to the end of my life.

She wiggles her nose with excitement. "I can't wait—won't it be lovely to be two married sisters together? Perhaps we'll get pregnant at the same time and share baby clothes—"

"You're jumping the gun again." I turn away and slip upstairs to my room. I try to wipe the pain off my face.

My bedroom drags me back into my teenage years. Stuffed animals squish together on my pillows, and books line the shelves. Everything is green paisley—the bedspread, curtains, and rug. My old clothes still hang in the closet. Bell-bottom jeans and satin jackets.

I comb my hair, sponge off in the bathroom, and apply lipstick and eyeliner. I squeeze into the black dress, which fits better now that I've lost more weight pining for Raja. I turn, half expecting to see my imaginary man watching me dress.

Muffled laughter and synthesized Indian pop music drift up through the floor. It's a wonder this kind of noise never bothered me when I lived here. We get used to things, and then we forget we got used to them.

I grab the V. S. Naipaul book, take a deep breath, and head downstairs, my fingers gripping the handrail, sweat breaking out in my armpits despite the washing and deodorant.

This is it. The moment I face my family.

The back room is crowded, the Hindi pop music growing louder. The whole gang is here—Ma and Auntie Kiki and

Kali and Durga, several Indian friends, colleagues from the university. Auntie Kiki's stooping and mild-mannered husband has a massive cigar hanging from his mouth. The party spills out through the French doors onto the veranda and into the backyard.

Then Kali comes whirling up to me, grinning. "I've found a new guy! Shagadelic. Met him at work."

"You always bounce back quickly." I hug her. "Where's Baba?"

"This way." She steers me through the crowd. Baba stands off in the distance, on the other side of the room, a million people crowding the space between us. He's smiling, a rare sight. Maybe his stock portfolio posted a gain today.

Auntie Kiki emerges like Godzilla in a green sari. "Lina, darling, how lovely to finally see you!" She rushes toward me, and I have the urge to duck, but then we meet in a head-on collision. Her airbag breasts cushion the impact. She hugs me, then releases, and I catch my breath and hope my ribs are still intact.

She glares at my head. "What have you done to your hair?"

"I drove with the window open, Auntie." My heart races. I know what's coming. The questions, the admonishments. "How was your flight from Kolkata?"

"Horrible, nah?" Auntie Kiki pulls me aside. "Turbulence

and cold. Ice-cold. Hardly anything to drink, and the food is terrible. Have you tried eating the airplane food?"

"It's horrible," I agree.

Her fingernails dig into my shoulders. "Lina, the engagement suits you well. You're looking pink-cheeked."

"Thanks, Auntie—"

"Don't thank me. Thank the stars. Thank the gods."

Then Baba comes up and gives me a hug. "My baby Lina has finally come. We've all been waiting."

"Happy birthday, Baba!" I kiss his cheek and put the V. S. Naipaul book on the table with the other wrapped gifts.

"Come!" Auntie steers me through the crowd, her elbows out. Everyone makes way, and I swear people are whispering about me.

"Auntie, I have to tell you something, about my engagement, about Raja—"

"Come come, no need to say—"

"No, I really must say." I raise my voice over the din of the stereo.

"You needn't. We know how much you have suffered waiting and waiting—"

"You don't understand, Auntie. You see, Raja and I—"

"Raja and you will live happily ever after!" Auntie leads me toward the door, and as the crowd parts, I grab her arm to keep steady. There, coming toward me in long, easy strides, is Raja Prasad.

Thirty-three

He looks striking in khaki pants and a white linen shirt. He takes me in his arms, sweeps me off my feet, and plants a firm kiss on my mouth. "My darling Lina. How I've missed you!"

The touch of his lips transports me to a glittering palace by the sea. I'm floating on a tide of bliss, then I pull back.

"What are you talking about? What's going on here?"

His eyes go cold, but his mouth is smiling. "So many weeks away from each other, and keeping such a secret from our families. How could we continue such a charade?"

"Raja, I—" I try to squirm from his grasp, but he holds me firmly around the waist.

"You've lost weight, Lina darling. Pining for me? I've been gone *so long*, I feared you may have forgotten me."

"How could she forget you?" Kali pipes up.

"How could I?" I smile, but the room goes watery.

"You must've gone crazy," he says between his teeth.

"Absolutely bonkers—"

"Don't speak. No need for words." Raja grins around at the room. Everyone grins back. The whole house drips joy and celebration. I can taste the giddy happiness. Kali's entire face is a smile, and Durga glows with approval.

My mouth moves, but words won't come out.

"I thought I'd surprise you," Raja says smoothly. "Thought I wasn't coming home until next week, did you?"

Kali claps. "He caught an early flight. He asked us to keep it a secret. Aren't you pleased, Lina?"

"Of course I'm pleased, but Auntie—"

"She's pleased." Raja winks at Auntie, as if they're the closest of friends. "She's most delightful. As are your parents."

Auntie pats my arm. "Why you would keep such a handsome prince a secret, we all don't know. You've done so well, my child. I can't wait to tell Pandit Parsai. How did you manage to steal Raja from the fiancée that all of India thought he had?"

"That *I* thought he had," I say, glancing up at him. Did he break up with the princess?

Auntie laughs. "You see!" She turns to the crowd. "My

niece was waiting for her perfect prince, and she has found him!"

Everyone claps. Roars.

"No, you don't understand—" I begin, but Raja interrupts.

"It is I who have done well." He spins me around. The crowd pulses with energy. In the doorway, Ma wipes a tear from the corner of her eye. How can I contaminate this joy?

"Do tell us more about your travels, Raja," Kali says. "Do you know, Lina, he told us the story of the biggest tiger in Bengal? He took pictures. You should see them. He went into the jungle on elephant back. He's so brave!"

"Indeed he is," Auntie says. "He's been entertaining us from the moment he arrived. Quite a man."

"Quite," I say with gratitude. Raja Prasad came to my rescue. He's my knight in shining armor, but his eyes glint like metal and he holds me in an iron grip.

"More Scotch?" Dad materializes with a glass in hand. "Raja has brought from duty-free. Thoughtful, nah?"

"Yes, how thoughtful," I say. The colors and shapes in the room waver and shimmer. I might faint.

Raja waves an arm. "Ah, Dr. Ray. I won't drink all your Glenlivet."

"We shall save some for next time!" Dad raises the glass.

"What's going on?" I whisper to Raja.

He whispers back between his teeth. "Not now, my love, while we're having so much fun."

"Your love?"

"You are as long as I say you are. Don't you remember our engagement?"

I yank my elbow away and smile at everyone while my chest implodes. Raja has knocked the breath out of me. How I wish it could be true. I want to be his love. I wish he didn't have a princess fiancée. I wish—

"There is much planning to be done!" Auntie shouts. "The gods are smiling upon us!"

"I know you want a big family wedding." Raja puts his arm around my shoulders. The repetitive drumbeat pounds up through my legs.

"We need to talk in private!" I turn to Raja. He grins. He's enjoying this!

"Here's to the happy couple!" Kali's cheeks flush, and her eyes shine. Her wine sloshes from the glass as she walks off-balance.

Raja kisses my hair. I can't wait to get him alone. If I make a scene here, my family will collapse like paper cutout dolls.

Auntie Kiki keeps nodding with approval, her toothy smile showing lipstick on her teeth.

Ma and Baba stand in the doorway, both smiling. Then someone turns up the music, and Raja spins me around, my mind turning and turning. "Let's dance, shall we? Everyone dance!"

We dance, and then a slow song comes on. Kali and Dev dance cheek to cheek, and Raja pulls me close.

"What are you doing?" I ask him.

"You wanted a fiancé named Raja, you got one."

"How long will you keep this up?"

"As long as I wish."

I press my hand to his muscular chest. "Thank you for coming to my rescue. I'm grateful, truly I am, but what will you say to your family? To the princess? Are you still engaged to her?"

"I have not yet made up my mind." He gazes down at me with a hungry look in his eyes.

I'm blushing again. "How did you know about Baba's birthday? How did you know to come here?"

"I spoke to Harry. He told me everything. I envy you for having such good friends, Lina. He believes in you."

My mouth goes dry. How I wish I could rewind time, meet Raja again and not lie, not say the things I said. "I was going to tell everyone the truth, but the more I tried, the deeper I fell into my own fibs."

"What the hell did you think you were doing, creating an imaginary fiancé with my name? Whom did you expect to marry?"

"I was dating men, trying to find one to fit the bill—"

"Nobody fit. I didn't fit. But you pretended I did."

"I had to think of a name fast—yours came up. Auntie wanted to set me up with Pee-wee. He's far from a suitable—"

"What's your *suitable* man? A fantasy?"

"Not anymore," I say. "What happens now?"

He narrows his gaze. "What do you want to have happen?"

For a crazy moment, I long to be alone in the world with Raja. Seeing him again is a ray of sunlight shining down through a long, black night. I want to strip away family, culture, the past. We stare at each other, the gulf closing between us, and then the distance unfolds again.

I take a deep breath. "I have to set the record straight. I have to undo my lies."

"Are you sure?" he asks, and his eyebrow rises.

"I have to." The song ends. I pull away from Raja and tug Ma's sleeve. "I need to talk to you and Baba in private. Now." My heart pounds, and my legs turn to rubber. Her face pales, but she nods, and we grab Baba, slip into the kitchen, and shut the door. Muffled music seeps in through the walls. The bright overhead light makes me squint.

"Ma, Baba, hear me out," I begin. "I have to tell you—"

"What is it? You're pregnant?" Ma asks, clasping her hands in front of her.

"No, nothing like that—"

"Is it Raja?" Baba asks. "Is he actually broke? Is he a gambler or—"

"No, Baba! Just listen."

Auntie bursts in, wineglass in hand. "What is this gathering? What secrets are being told?"

Kali rushes in after her. "I saw you all trying to sneak in here without me. What's going on?"

Durga follows, and my parents, two sisters, and auntie stand staring at me, their eyes wide with expectation.

No turning back now.

"Back in India, at Durga's wedding, I told a lie," I say. "I made up a fake fiancé. He wasn't real."

"Oh, Vishnu," Auntie whispers.

"Raja and I met at Durga's wedding, but we weren't dating." Auntie stands with the palm of her hand over her chest, as if to keep her heart from spilling out.

"I came home without a fiancé, but I realized then, after seeing Durga so happy, after returning to an empty apartment, that I really did want a partner in life. And I love you all so much—" I glance at Ma, Durga, Kali. "I couldn't let you down. But how would I find a suitable man? Who would he be? After Nathu, nobody lived up to my ideal. I tried dating. No luck."

Auntie screams. "Oh, Vishnu, what has happened?"

"Auntie, hush!" Kali puts an arm around her shoulders, and Durga pats Auntie's back. Ma's face is ashen. Baba keeps blinking.

I forge on, relate my attempts to maintain the charade,

my meetings with Raja. I spill every fear, every truth I never told, from my attempts to come clean, to my dates with Pramit, Dr. Dutta, and Patrick. My eyes brim with tears, and I try to ignore the expressions of horror crossing the faces of my family members. Baba looks crumpled, as if he's just unpacked himself from a suitcase. Ma leans against the countertop. She plays with her hair, kneading it like dough. Auntie goes stiff, lips pressed together in a white line.

I keep on talking, professing my love for my family, the joy I saw in their faces when they thought I was engaged.

Baba removes his glasses and rubs his forehead. Two red indentations are left on either side of his nose, where the glasses pressed into the skin. "Such an elaborate deception. How can this be? What have you done?"

"I didn't want to get married, and I felt pressure," I say. "But that's no excuse. The whole thing snowballed out of control."

"Nobody has ever pressured you!" Ma bursts out.

"What do you mean, nobody has ever pressured me? Weddings are a huge event in India. Every woman aspires to nothing more than the perfect marriage to the perfect man. Even Kali! All starry-eyed. And Auntie Kiki too."

"Lina, what on earth!" Auntie's cheeks puff outward. "What nonsense are you saying?"

"What about me?" Durga said. "Do you think I was only responding to pressure?"

"Of course not." I touch her cheek. "You're so lucky to have found true love."

Kali glowers at me. "I'll find love too. There's nothing wrong with being starry-eyed."

A guest wanders in with a beer bottle in his hand. We all glare at him, and he turns around and scampers out again.

"If you don't want marriage, Lina, you needn't marry!" Ma says, but her trembling lips say otherwise.

"So little has changed in India," I say. "Cell phones, the Internet, Coca-Cola, none of that means anything. The social structure of India hasn't changed much, Ma. And you and Baba glowed with pride when Durga was hitched. Don't tell me you don't care if I don't marry!"

"Lina, enough," Baba says. "Why you've deceived us, I don't know. Our family reputation has been tarnished."

"I was looking at saris," Ma says in a plaintive voice. "Kiki was consulting the astrologer. We were looking for a good place for the marriage. I was thinking of grandchildren."

"I'm so sorry, Ma," I say.

"What everyone must think of us," she whispers.

Raja strides in, and a sharp longing scrapes across my chest. He's familiar to me now. The way he stands with his broad shoulders squared, the scent of his cologne, his long legs, his black eyes urging me on. "Am I interrupting?" he asks, taking in our tense faces.

Baba rubs the indentations on his nose. "What Lina's saying makes no sense. She dates you, she pretends to be engaged, and now she's saying none of this was real."

"I screwed up, and I'm sorry," I say. "You all deserve better. Raja deserves better." I give him a wan smile. "He came here tonight to help me save face, and for that, I'm grateful. I truly care for him. I've learned he's a good man. It's crazy and stupid, and things can never work out between us, but—"

"You see," Raja says. "I'm betrothed to another, although I've not made my final decision. I care very much for Lina—"

"But Raja and I come from different worlds. I can't imagine living in India. I have a job here, my friends, my life—"

"—and I have my life in India. I can't abandon my family," Raja says, "or my work."

Nobody speaks, and then Uncle Gula wanders in, an unlit cigar dangling from his lips. "I wondered where you'd all gone off to."

The kitchen is crowded now. So much for a private talk with Ma and Baba. Music and laughter tumble in from the living room, and then Auntie throws up her hands. "Oh, Vishnu! Lina lives in America, Raja lives in India. So what? You're in love! Any fool can see. Young people in the modern world, they want to have it all. This problem, that problem. Always complaining. In our day, we crossed galaxies to be together. You must not give up so easily."

I stare at her, all the protests stuck in my throat.

"Did you know your uncle and me, we came from different states, and we are six years apart in age? His parents disapproved of the match." Auntie hooks her arm through Uncle's elbow. He pats his balding head.

"We escaped to see each other without telling our parents," Auntie goes on. "And then we traveled together to Delhi—"

"It was fun, nah?" Uncle smiles at Auntie, plants a kiss on her forehead. "Such a time on the train." Their gazes tangle in a loving embrace.

"Auntie's right," Ma says. "Why all this nonsense? Your Baba and I have been married thirty-five years, and at times we want to kill each other."

"*Most* of the time we want to kill each other," Baba says, wrapping his arms around Ma.

"And yet we stay together, and our love grows deeper," she says.

"Why must the world be in black and white?" Auntie shouts. "Young people, all the time wanting perfection. You want always new clothes, new cars, the perfect arrangements."

"Life is messy," Ma says. "What stories I could tell. Before I met your Baba, I was engaged to the maharajah of—"

"O-ho, enough!" Baba cuts in. "They don't want to know of your prior romantic escapades."

Auntie waggles a finger at Raja and me. "You find a way to work things out. At least you must try."

"You're always saying long-distance relationships don't

work," Kali says. "They can, if you want them to. You have to try."

"Have you met his family?" Auntie asks.

Raja and I shake our heads at the same time.

"Oh, Vishnu! Then we'll revise your plans. Go to India—"

"I can't go again, Auntie. I've just been—"

"You must go," Durga says.

"Yes, you must come." Raja takes my hand. His fingers are warm and firm, sending a pulse of electricity through me. He turns to my family. "I've already invited Lina to visit my mother and me in our house in Puri. I'll pay for the journey."

Auntie Kiki nods, her toothy smile confirming her approval.

"What do you say, Lina?" Raja takes my other hand and gazes into my eyes. My insides go watery again. Meet his mother? Visit his home in Puri?

"Another wild family adventure," I say, glancing around at the cluster of relatives. "How can I refuse?"

Thirty-four

*A*untie Kiki and I are shopping on Kolkata's Jawaharlal Nehru Road, still known by its older name, Chowringhee Road. The sky must have grown tired of oppressing the city, for now it opens to welcome a cool autumn breeze. Clouds tumble overhead, and a slight drizzle dampens my skin.

We thread our way through a seething crowd of shoppers, past pavement vendors selling everything from water pistols to underwear, carpets to handicrafts. We finally reach New Market, a bustling commercial hub. Merchants sell caneware, silk saris, silver jewelry, incense, sculptures, and souvenirs.

Auntie chooses several saris and haggles with a vendor. "Lina, see? This red one will be perfect for your visit with Raja's ma," she says.

"Red is a wedding color, Auntie. I'm not ready for that. I'm just meeting her, not—"

"I know how difficult it is for you to come to India." She puts down the saris and moves on to the next booth. "The crowds bother you, the noise. You have few memories here. And you don't know how to bargain, nah? You buy everything at face value—"

"You're very perceptive, Auntie, but I'm okay."

"You're not okay. I know this. Your past is not here. Listen, now. Hush."

Across the road, a woman sings a sweet, lilting melody. *"Mendichya panavar man ajoon jhulatai ga."*

"What does it mean?" I ask, watching the woman unroll tapestries on the sidewalk.

"My heart still meanders on the leaves of henna," Auntie says.

I'll never know the ache of memory behind such words. And yet, I can't help but hope that I'll find some element of home in Puri.

"Welcome to our home by the sea." Raja takes my hand. His fingers are firm and warm, and a thrill rushes through me at his touch. My hair is a mess again, and I'm covered in dust and sweat and feeling slightly nauseated from the three-hour drive over winding, bumpy roads.

"This place is lovely." I look up the marble steps toward a sprawling house with open archways and big windows, right at the edge of a white-sand beach on the Bay of Bengal. I smell the sea's wild saltiness. Raja, dressed in jeans and a casual shirt, helps me up the steps. He's the perfect gentleman.

At the top stands a sparrowlike woman in jeans and a sweater. Her silken gray hair hangs loose, moving in the breeze. She's beautiful, the weather of years settling comfortably into her features.

"Lina, this is my mother, Neelu Prasad."

I'll topple backward down the steps and faint in the sand. "Your mother?"

"It's a pleasure to meet you." She speaks in a steady, cultured voice, unassuming and soft.

She's holding out her hand. I take it—her fingers feel bony as bird claws, and cool. Perhaps it's age, or perhaps she has always been this delicate. Difficult to imagine that a man as big as Raja Prasad could be the son of such a small woman.

I let go of her hand and smile.

"Please, come in," she says. "You must be hungry and thirsty after such a long journey." She leads me into an open-air living room, sparsely furnished with modest couches and tables. Books line the massive shelves, and I have the urge to search the volumes, some of which look older than this house. The faint smell of sandalwood incense comes from another room, and wind chimes play a soft melody in the distance.

We sit on the couches, and a silent servant breezes in, dressed in white. Mrs. Prasad expresses her wishes with a nod, and the servant disappears. A silent language has passed between them.

"Your house is lovely," I say. "Thanks for having me."

"We're delighted," Neelu Prasad says as the servant brings tea. The China teapot and cups are wafer-thin, probably rare, the tray beneath made of intricately carved brass.

"Lina, please understand," Neelu goes on. "Our home is your home. You're welcome to stay. You'll let us know if you need anything, won't you?"

"You're very kind." I try to imagine what life would be like here in Puri, or in the Kolkata house or the cottage in Santiniketan. "How often do you come to Puri?"

"When Raja has time to bring me," Neelu says. "His business is mainly in Kolkata."

"Stone exporting, I know. But I don't know much else." I glance at Raja, who leans back on the couch, his feet on the table. He's wearing *chappals*, Indian sandals. He's entirely at ease. An ache squeezes my heart. How I long to feel at home here, and yet the ocean breeze, the shouts of fishermen or vendors in the distance, the sunlight diffused by ocean spray, still feel foreign.

"What do you want to know?" Raja opens his hands toward me. "My business is called Granite Point. I have many associates who manage the details. We export, wholesale, and retail Indian marble, slate, and granite. We offer many designs and types of products—"

"*Acha*, Raja," Neelu says. "Lina couldn't possibly be interested—"

"I'm fascinated."

"Raja tells me you're quite accomplished in your field. Matchmaking is a difficult endeavor."

I glance sidelong at Raja. He doesn't blink. "I—haven't been too good at it lately."

"Raja says you're the best."

"What about you? Raja says you're quite accomplished," I say.

"Hah, I taught physics in college for several years, but I've recently retired. You live an independent life in San Francisco. How I should love to visit."

"Then you should." I want to tell her she can have my apartment, sleep in my bed, and I'll cook Indian food for her, even though my cooking sucks.

"I should love that." She smiles warmly.

Then I see the kitten, now a big, furry cat, curled up on a settee in the corner. The cat Raja rescued.

I smile, and we talk for a long time, until the tea is cold and the pot nearly empty. I learn about Raja's mishaps as a child, the time a cobra nearly bit him, the night he sleep-walked and nearly drowned in the sea. I learn of his first girl-friend, a British girl visiting from London with her nanny.

"I caught them kissing in the bathroom," Mrs. Prasad says, and Raja's face reddens. I've never seen him blush.

As the sun dips toward the horizon, a red glow seeps across the sky.

"Go on for a walk," Neelu says, getting up. "I'm off to find the cook."

I stand, my legs stiff. My heartbeat picks up at the prospect of walking on the beach with Raja again. Will he drag me into the surf? He takes my hand and leads me down the marble steps to the beach. We walk barefoot next to the shoreline. After the crowds of Kolkata, the deserted stretch of white sand calms my nerves, and for a few moments I forget that this man still might choose the princess. A thick, salty breeze rolls in from the sea.

"You never told me how you got the scar on your cheek," I say. "I've been picturing a battle or sword fight—"

Raja laughs. "You're a woman of imagination. In reality, the story is much more mundane. I was a child playing croco-dile with Dev. We would jump from bed to bed to avoid the 'crocodiles' lurking on the floor. I missed the mattress and hit my face on the bedpost instead. My mother was beside her-self. The wound required six stitches."

"I bet you didn't cry." I grin at him.

"I bawled like a baby, despite my mother's attempts to comfort me." He walks close, still holding my hand.

"She's not what I expected. I thought she'd be bossy and loud, like Auntie."

"My mother doesn't push," he says.

"She has an inner glow, a kind of peace."

"So do you, at times." Raja squeezes my fingers. "I wish you could feel at home here, Lina, but I see the ambivalence in your eyes. In this global world, people e-mail each other across great distances, and yet we're still light-years apart."

"I can't help who I am, Raja. I grew up in the States. I watched *Sesame Street* and played with Lite Brite and Spiro-Tot. We didn't celebrate all the Indian festivals. We had Santa Claus and Thanksgiving and Christmas trees with ornaments."

"I'd like to learn about Thanksgiving—what is it? You slaughter large chickens, is it?"

"Turkeys. I don't eat them, but many people do. Still, I like the holiday. It's one of the few days without traffic, when most of the stores are closed and people visit family and stuff their faces with food, and then everyone complains that they've gained too much weight and they go on whirlwind diets that don't work."

"*Acha*—you know your country, as I know mine. My father ran Granite Point for several years. The business faltered, but now it's doing well. And the orphanages need me.

There's still much work to be done. I'm loath to leave my projects."

"I'd never want you to leave your projects," I say. "Your roots are here."

"And so are yours."

"My roots may be here, but my home is there." I point west across the distance.

Sunset spreads over the sand, bathing Puri in a rose-tinted glow. If only we could remain here, suspended in twilight.

Raja stops and takes my face in his hands, forcing me to gaze up into his eyes. The unspoken words *Princess Sayantoni* hover between us. The princess understands Raja's culture. With her, he would never have to travel; never have to forsake his home.

How can this faint silver filament, the spectral thread reaching from my heart to his, ever bridge the continents between us?

Thirty-five

I'm sitting at my computer in a bedroom so big and desolate it could be a foreign country. Since I returned to San Francisco, the fog hasn't lifted. Morning mist slithers through the city, flicking its tongue into every corner, breathing through windows. In my sleep, the haze hypnotizes me, lulls me into complacency. Americans don't worry about frequent power cuts or whether leftovers will rot in the fridge. We don't thank the shower for producing clean water with the proper pressure. After two weeks in India, *I* do. I worship water. I immerse myself in bubble baths until my toes shrivel into prunes.

I'm writing Raja an e-mail to thank him for paying my way to India, for taking care of me in Puri. I extend my warmest gratitude to his mother. Her mild rice and *dahl* nourished me through illness. I hope the arthritis is better in her thumbs. I'll never again take opposable thumbs for granted.

When I threw up for two days, Raja held a cool compress to my forehead, brought me lime-flavored Electral, an electrolyte drink, to restore my strength. I still smell his spicy cologne, hear his comforting, steady voice. He read to me from the Ramayana, the epic story of Rama and his great love, Sita. When the ten-headed demon, Ravana, kidnapped Sita, Rama amassed an army to rescue her.

Now I understand what Raja's life means to him in India. Here, life is television. *Survivor, CSI: Crime Scene Investigation, Law & Order.* The flickering tube can all too easily suck us into its virtual world. I came home and I was startled by a sense of emptiness, although traffic chokes the highways. Even in the city, there's a sense of isolation. We don't understand population density the way Kolkatans understand it.

Here, there's room for everyone, and no resource will ever run out. That's what we think, anyway, and I wonder if we take too much for granted as we pop hairspray and DVDs into metal carts and stand in line at the checkout.

What struck me most, upon returning this time, was the layer of flesh between skin and bone, giving Americans the appearance of smooth jointlessness. I remembered, with a sharp ache, the sinew and flat, lean muscle on every rickshaw-wallah, roadside vendor, and servant in India. What a demarcation between rich and poor.

The day Raja and I returned to Kolkata, we took an auto-rickshaw through the streets, and I had no idea where we were going. We stopped to witness a demonstration. Factory workers were on strike. They sat cross-legged in the dirt, chanting, waving their arms, but I couldn't understand the language. Silly me.

We moved on and presently arrived at the Save the Children orphanage. I didn't know Raja was funding the house renovations. My heart lifted when I smelled fresh paint in two of the rooms. My small donations to charities paled in comparison. What had I been doing with my life? The girls laughed, fresh in their clean dresses, some in white-and-blue uniforms. Anchala, a tribal girl, trotted up and took my hand. Her fingers were warm. She spoke broken English, asked about my Liz Claiborne jeans. I wanted to take them off and give them to her. She was missing a front tooth, and I thought, the tooth fairy won't leave a quarter under her pillow, so I gave her a quarter, and she just looked at it and smiled. The silver glinted in the sun. For her, the quarter was nature's artifact, like a shining rock one might find on the beach. She wasn't thinking of what she could buy—bubble gum or jellybeans. While Raja went inside to talk to the director, Anchala and the girls and I played in the courtyard, surrounded by a crumbling red brick wall. The climbing clematis lent wildness to the garden, and I thought if I found a loose brick in the wall, I could open a door to a better world. I would transport the girls, and for those who'd been abandoned simply because they were girls, I would grant a new set of loving parents.

There's still so much to fix. A new pathway from the road to the orphanage, from the back way, needs to be constructed. The ponds need embankments. The children's rooms need renovations. Now I know why Raja wanted a woman who could care for his family. What he really wanted was a woman who could help him care for the lost and forgotten.

I say all this in my e-mail, in the hope that Raja will see another side of me, too. I sign the letter, *Love, Lina* and send it off into cyberspace.

In the evening, there's a message from Raja:

Dearest Lina,
Thank you for your kind letter. I hope this finds you well. I must apologize for not replying sooner. I've been in Mumbai soliciting funds for a new school for girls in Karagpur. The home in Thakurpukur will receive state support, for which I am grateful. I also paid a visit to the local bustee welfare center. We're

planning a few new vocational training projects.

I'm home now and enjoying some respite with Ma. She read your letter with eagerness. Her thumbs have improved. She can't stop speaking of you. Somehow, you managed to enchant the girls at Save the Children. Their lives have been rough, with so few reasons for joy, and you made them happy.

Anchala took a special liking to you. She draws pictures of you, and I suspect you're her surrogate mother. Ma has explained several times that you live in America, but Anchala does not yet understand these vast distances. Either you live next door, or you live on Pluto. I told her America is much closer to Pluto, and her face fell.

I've thought often of you since you left, and I must confess, I dream of you often.

Raja

I close the e-mail with a sharp sense of loss. Twilight whispers pink across the horizon, and I find myself missing daylight. *I dream of you.* If only these fantasies, these imaginings fashioned from stardust and longing—if only these dreams could come true.

Thirty-six

San Francisco is clear today. Along the western horizon, the waterline cuts the sky. I taste the cold, clean air on my way to work, and my mind is sharp when Mr. Sen arrives for his appointment at ten o'clock.

"Would you like some tea?" I ask.

"You've never offered." He sits, looking flustered.

"I know, and I apologize. We have Earl Grey, Breakfast Blend, Darjeeling—"

"Darjeeling, thank you!"

After I bring him tea, we talk about his plans.

"America is a vast land of opportunity, but you drive for

227

miles and never meet a soul," he says. "I have no family here, no prospects for marriage."

I rest my elbows on the desk, my chin in my hands. "I know what it feels like to be alone. I know what it's like to be confused, to . . . feel the need to live up to someone else's expectations."

Mr. Sen leans back, as if my words were a blast of wind. We're both silent for a time.

"My parents expected me to make something of myself here," he says finally. "To pursue the American dream and send money home, and most of all, they expected me to bring home a wife."

"You *have* made something of yourself here. I'm sure your parents are proud." I still taste the sea air in Puri, still hear Raja's mother talking in her soft voice. Restlessness pulls at my insides.

The corners of his mouth turn down. "I'm beginning to love Starbucks, nah? And the Fisherman's Wharf. I have dinner at Gaylord's India Restaurant once a week, and I know the chef. I want to stay in America, but now my parents want me to return to India."

"Maybe we can keep trying. Give me another chance. That's why I called you here today. I won't charge you."

"No, I can't allow you to work for nothing."

"I want to help—"

"You've done all you can do. Please."

"Are you sure? I—"

"Don't fret. All will work itself out."

We stand and shake hands. He has a firm grip, surprising for such a slight man, but then, I'm no longer so easily surprised.

My heart heavy, I walk him out to the waiting room, where Mrs. Mukerjee paces with her usual impatience, her daughter sitting on the couch, her nose in *People Magazine*. She wears an invisible bubble around her.

As Mr. Sen walks by, I see it.

"Stop!" I shout.

He rests his hand on the doorknob. He turns around, startled.

"Wait, you forgot something." I rush to put myself between him and the door.

"What? I've got my hat, my wallet—"

"Just a minute." I yank Sonya to her feet. The silvery filament extends from her chest to Mr. Sen's chest—well, actually, it catches on the hem of her sari and hangs there, the thread slackening as I pull her closer to him.

"Mr. Sen, I'd like you to meet Miss Sonya Mukerjee." I join their hands, and the colors fuse in an aura of light. Sonya looks up at him, and their gazes lock, and we're tumbling through a romantic movie. Roses bloom in time-lapse photography, and clouds race across the sky as Mr. Sen and Miss Mukerjee exchange the usual pleasantries—*lovely to meet you,*

How are you. Their minds and bodies are already leaning into the future.

Mrs. Mukerjee's face puckers. I take her by the elbow and swing her into my office.

"Mr. Sen comes from a good family, much money, very smart, Brahmin, very nice and caring," I say quickly, and I keep talking, all my skills back again, and as I talk, Mrs. Mukerjee relaxes.

"I always thought he would make a good husband," she says. "He's always leaving when we're coming in, and I'm looking at him and thinking, Now, that man may be the right man for my daughter."

I give her the credit. "Yes, you made a good match."

"Of course, you may keep the money. After all, they met here."

"You're very kind."

After they leave, chattering, the glow still coming at me under the door, I go into Donna's office.

She looks up. "He called."

My heart leaps. "And?"

I sit across from her, take in the curved lines of her face, the porcelain tone of her skin, the papers on her desk, the scent of floral perfume, the little Beanie Babies lined up next to her computer, the pictures of her son and Dev. She and Dev are engaged, and he plans to stay on in the States. These anchors keep her here, give her life meaning.

She reads the question in my expression. "Raja wants to talk to you. He has news. He thought it best to let you know."

"Let me know what?"

She shrugs, sadness in her eyes. "He didn't say. He'll call you at home tonight."

I know what Raja will say. He and the princess have set a wedding date. I go home to wait.

Thirty-seven

The call comes through a little after nine. The line is unnaturally clear, as if Raja's breathing into my ear. I imagine he has just woken up to a cool morning by the sea.

"I need to tell you something," he says. "I want you to keep everything you hold dear. Your job, your friends, your family."

He's preparing me for the inevitable news of his engagement to Princess Sayantoni. "Thank you, Raja. I wish the same for you."

"I've made my choice."

"What choice?" I whisper, although I already know the answer.

"I did some soul-searching in Puri, after you left, and . . . I'm applying for another visa."

"You what?" Time slows again, the wall clock ticking away the hour in long seconds.

"I'm coming to America. I need to get to know you better. I need a lover, a best friend. Perhaps a wife, but we'll see."

The room tilts, his words rushing at me. "Raja—"

"Don't speak." I imagine him putting a finger to my lips. I watch the angle of light coming in through the window, the smells, the sounds of my city. I love San Francisco. I love my family. I love my friends. Raja loves all the same things in India, but he's willing to give up everything he holds dear to be with me. I imagine I'm right next to him, feeling his heartbeat, the warmth of his skin, the solid silver thread shimmering between us.

Thirty-eight

$\mathcal{I}$'m on the afternoon train leaving Kolkata's Howrah Station. I'm not sure where this journey will end. I try to read the *Statesman* newspaper, but it's hard to concentrate.

Finally, the steam train hisses and groans away from the station, and my heart sings with anticipation. I hold Star Galaxy in my hand for good luck. My home remains in San Francisco, but I'm widening my net, as Harry would say. When I was born, Pandit Parsai predicted I'd search for love across many seas. He was right.

I unfold the glossy India brochure. On this trip, I'll visit the Taj Mahal and sink my toes into the hot, white sands of

Goa. First, I'll meet Raja in Puri, then attend the opening ceremony of his new school for girls in Karagpur. Anchala will
be there. She'll grow up and become someone, and maybe
one day she'll travel to San Francisco.

I close my eyes and picture the city, Coit Tower rising into
the clouds. My mind races out to Marin County, Mendocino,
Point Reyes National Seashore, gray whales spouting in the
distant sea.

Later, as the sky darkens, the train coasts to a stop. I step
onto the platform. The crowds move in, and then a tall man
strides toward me. There's a hush, as if the earth has fallen
into silence as Raja embraces me.

"Are you lost, ma'am?" He takes my face in his hands.

"I came to see the stars at twilight," I whisper, gazing into
his eyes. "Did you know there are three different moments of
twilight? Civil twilight, nautical twilight, and astronomical
twilight?"

"Is that so? Which one is happening now?" A smile
touches his lips.

"Nautical twilight. General outlines are still visible, but
the horizon is indistinct—"

"You remember well."

"I also remembered Star Galaxy." I press the stone into his
hand. "It belongs here, in its home by the sea."

He tucks the stone into his pocket, then he kisses my forehead, my eyebrows, my cheeks. "I was afraid you wouldn't

come. I was afraid you'd find the perfect man of your dreams, and he wouldn't be me."

"How could you think such a thing?" I whisper. "You're better than any man I can imagine."

I glance back toward the train. A shadow-face appears in the window, my imaginary man who was once Nathu. He's barely a wisp of a shape as he raises his hand to wave good-bye.

Up Close and Personal with the Author

HOW DID THE IDEA FOR THIS STORY COME TO YOU?

I learned of a cousin's wedding in India and imagined standing squished in a crowd of relatives in a hot Kolkata courtyard. I wondered how I would feel. Fascinated? Happy to be with family? Completely disoriented?

The rest of the story followed quickly. Lina's far more audacious than I am—I would never invent an imaginary man!

OH, REALLY? THEN HOW DO YOU EXPLAIN RAJA PRASAD?

You caught me! I guess I do have a fertile imagination. When the Pee-wee Herman clone practically drooled on Lina, I couldn't help rescuing her. The handsome, debonair Raja popped out of my—I mean Lina's—head.

HAVE YOU KNOWN A MAN LIKE RAJA? WHERE DID YOU FIND HIM?

He's a composite of every dashing man I've seen in the movies. He's inscrutable (Keanu Reeves), rough-edged (Tommy Lee Jones), sophisticated (George Clooney), sexy (Brad Pitt), and dangerous (Christian Bale), with a touch of the exotic. Phew! As Lina would say, he's Vin Diesel with hair.

IF WE SAT IN A RESTAURANT, COULD YOU IDENTIFY SHIMMERING THREADS BETWEEN POTENTIAL MATES?

I'd be a terrible matchmaker—I couldn't see a shimmering love thread if someone dangled one in front of my face. I grew up immersed in science and the laws of physics. My father is a chemical engineer and my mother has a doctorate in science and math education. I broke the mold by studying anthropology and psychology and then pursuing the arts.

WHICH ASPECTS OF YOUR LIFE CORRESPOND TO LINA'S?

I was born in India, but I grew up in Canada. Most of the novel takes place in the San Francisco Bay Area, where I lived for several years after graduating from U.C. Berkeley. I struggled through many boyfriends before finding my husband.

We now live in the Pacific Northwest with three cats, a rabbit, and plenty of surrounding wildlife.

DO YOU FEEL THE SAME CONFLICT BETWEEN CULTURES?

In some ways, yes. I was one of only a few Indian kids growing up in a Manitoba town. Although I made close friends there, a couple of small-minded bullies called me names. I didn't always feel comfortable in my brown skin.

I also felt out of place when we visited Indian families whose children spoke their mother tongue. My parents sometimes spoke in Bengali to each other, but they never taught me Bengali.

Yet Indian culture infused our lives. My parents were affectionate and demonstrative, as Indian families often are, while my friends rarely hugged or kissed their parents. My parents cooked Bengali food, had close Indian friends, and we returned to India a few times. On weekend mornings we lounged in our pajamas and drank chai (Indian tea with lots of milk and sugar). When I stayed overnight at friends' houses, I found it strange that everyone got dressed to have a formal breakfast together. What, no tea in bed??

Now that I've moved out and established my own life, I have a better understanding of my unusual family background, and I don't feel much conflict between cultures. I feel like a North American, and yet I'm also proud of my Indian heritage.

YOUR FAMILY DIDN'T TRY TO ARRANGE YOUR MARRIAGE?

Heck no! My family is much more unconventional than Lina's. My parents fell in love; their marriage was not arranged. They were adventurous, the first members of their family to seek an independent life in a foreign country.

As such, they emphasized education and encouraged me to excel in my studies, piano lessons, figure skating, swimming, and ballet. Nobody bothered me about getting married until one day, when I broke up with a longtime boyfriend, my mother let slip, "Now you'll never get married!"

HOW MANY INDIAN WEDDINGS HAVE YOU ATTENDED?

None actually in India, but I recall a traditional Indian wedding in Canada that was packed with relatives, friends, and children running everywhere. The beautiful bride, decked out in gold jewelry and a red silk sari, trembled with anxiety. Before the ceremony, she ran to the bathroom and threw up.

Within India, there are many different types of wedding

traditions. The movie *Monsoon Wedding* depicts a typical upper middle-class Punjabi wedding, while the wedding in *Imaginary Men* is Brahmo Samaj, a more reserved Bengali affair.

A few months ago, I attended my Bengali cousin's wedding in Denver, Colorado. She married an American man from a Roman Catholic family. The couple and a few friends later flew to Kolkata, India, for the Bengali version of the wedding.

THE SCENES SET IN KOLKATA ARE SENSUOUS AND VIVID. DID YOU DO RESEARCH TO CREATE SUCH A SEEMINGLY AUTHENTIC SENSE OF PLACE OR DID YOU RELY ON FIRSTHAND EXPERIENCE?

While I did some research to sharpen the details, I relied mainly on firsthand experience. I was born in Kolkata—then called Calcutta—and I've returned a few times. A complex, energetic city, Kolkata conjures images of crumbling colonial facades, enchanting beauty, culture, chaotic crowds, traffic, squalor, poverty. Everyone who's been there has to agree—Kolkata is unforgettable.

THE RELATIONSHIPS BETWEEN LINA AND HER SISTERS, DURGA AND KALI, RING WONDERFULLY TRUE. DO YOU HAVE SISTERS?

I'm the eldest of five children in a rather unusual family. When I was four, we adopted my younger sister, Nita, from a Cree reservation in northern Manitoba, Canada. She's the other kind of Indian—Native American.

After my parents divorced and remarried, my father and his Italian wife had a son and adopted two daughters from India. They spend the school year in California and holidays in Italy. So I have three Italian-speaking Indo-American siblings and one Native American sister. Our cultures are all over the map.

WHEN DID YOU START WRITING?

As a child, I typed stories, stapled the pages together, and pasted copyright notices inside the front covers. I guess I inherited my grandmother's love of writing fiction. An English author, she married a Bengali man and moved to India. My mother grew up in Kolkata. When my grandmother visited us in Canada, she pretended to edit my drafts. She just scribbled a note here and there in the margin.

WHAT ARE YOU WORKING ON NOW?

I'm working on an unusual love story, set in Seattle, featuring an Indo-American woman who lives a clandestine, double life. That's all I can say. It's a secret! Stay tuned!

There's nothing better than the perfect bag...

Unless it's the perfect book.